The Time
of
Pedro

OTHER NOVELS BY JOE COHEN

BILLBOARDS
(1985)

THE MYSTERY OF EVE
(1995)

OAKLAND GLIMMER &
TALES OF THE WANT ADS
(2000)

THE MINEFIELD
(2002)

WANDERING CAIN
(2007)

THE RABBI & PRINCESS HARMONICA
(2012)

The Time of Pedro

of

Pedro

Joe Cohen

REGENT PRESS
Berkeley, California
2021

[paper-back]
ISBN 13: 978-1-58790-584-1
ISBN 10: 1-58790-584-1

[e-book]
ISBN 13: 978-1-58790-586-5
ISBN 10: 1-58790-586-8

Library of Congress Cataloging-in-Publication Data

Names: Cohen, Joe, 1934- author.
Title: The time of pedro / Joe Cohen.
Description: First edition. | Berkeley, California : Regent Press, 2021. |
    Summary:
Identifiers: LCCN 2021044863 (print) | LCCN 2021044864 (ebook) | ISBN
    9781587905841 (paper-back) | ISBN 1587905841 (paper-back) | ISBN
    9781587905865 (e-book) | ISBN 1587905868 (e-book)
Classification: LCC PS3603.O42432 T56 2021 (print) | LCC PS3603.O42432
    (ebook) | DDC 813/.6--dc23
LC record available at https://lccn.loc.gov/2021044863
LC ebook record available at https://lccn.loc.gov/2021044864

First Edition

The drawing of the author on the back cover is by Pete Najarian.

Graphic design by Mark Weiman.

Manufactured in the U.S.A.
REGENT PRESS
Berkeley, California
www.regentpress.net

Let not mercy and truth forsake you; bind them around your neck, write them on the tablet of your heart.
— PROVERBS 3:3

Part One

POLAND

Pedro Stefanek was convicted of blasphemy, black magic and false prophecy on April 15,1492 by a tribunal of the Spanish Inquisition and sentenced to burn at the stake at Valencia on May 30, his birthday.

Luckily, Doña Adelina, wife of the prison director, had other plans. Not one to be easily fooled, she was certain of Pedro's divine appointment as savior of the world. When she gazed at a drawing of his face, tears filled her eyes, she flushed, and she would touch her breasts. She was not going to let this saintly man perish in flames.

So it happened that Pedro found a note tucked in a chunk of bread ten days before the impending auto da fe:

"Do not despair. You will be saved."

He ate the bread, shredded the note, tossed it into the dung bucket, and did a little dance. He slept soundly that night for the first time since his arrest.

Rabbi Abiel Cardoza told his congregants in a synagogue in Almeria that Pedro Stefanek was a defiled Jew, a teacher of lies, an eyesore before God, and that his accursed name should be erased from the book of life and never again mentioned by righteous men and women.

Fray Tomas de Torquemada, Grand Inquisitor of Spain, told an overflowing crowd at the Cathedral of Segovia that Pedro Stefanek's immolation would be a great advance in the struggle against Satan, and urged all present to remain alert for enemies of the Church and report them to the Holy Office.

Ahmed Revaz, Moorish poet and soldier, wrote to his friend:

"Pedro,

The perception that people are joined in one divine creation regardless of dogma will take root and live beyond us and our troubled time. You've swum against a tide of foolishness, my friend. —Ahmed"

Pedro's mother Sara, wrapped in a blanket, slept beneath a tree outside the prison.

She awoke as doves serenaded the light of dawn, happy to hear their song and smell the damp grass. Wakefulness increased, thoughts returned, and she was miserable again.

When Sara was a child she lived in a village in Poland with her parents and her younger brother Aron. Except for a state deputy and his family, the hundred and fifty residents of the village Kletki were Jews. They tilled a modest expanse of land that produced vegetables and grain and they cultivated fruit trees and raised livestock. There was a blacksmith, a cooperative of fixers and builders, an accountant, a physician who saw to animals as well as humans, and there was Rabbi Elias Kline, who guided the villagers along the path of righteousness. His court consisted of nine scholars called rebs, four of them well versed in the intricacies of torah, the other five, less so.

Sara's father Daniel Brodky, a woodcarver, found the study of scripture mildly interesting but not very compelling. Along with his carving, he spent time riding, hunting, roaming the Carpathians, and drinking vodka. Occasionally, he worked as a hunting guide for Polish or Lithuanian noblemen.

After his wife died of pneumonia, vodka became a necessity. Some said it was his second marriage.

Esther, the mama, died when Sara was twelve, and Aron seven. Delirious with fever, she hallucinated a ballet of angels, stars, and her family swirling in the brilliant January sky. She slid feebly out of bed drenched in sweat, crawled out the door and lay on the snow watching the celestial drama come to an end. Near dawn, Daniel reached for her and discovered she was gone. He ran outside in terror, found her frozen and lifeless, carried her inside, covered her, begged her to live, but she was beyond pleas and tears.

After the funeral, Daniel left the children with his brother's family, disappeared, and returned after ten days with a slash on his forehead, torn clothing, and specks of dried blood on his beard.

"You want to know where I've been." The family, seated at breakfast, waited.

"I've been drunk and now I'm sober and we will resume our lives."

He embraced Aron and Sara, took their hands, and they walked home.

A variety of speculations spread through the village regarding Daniel's lost days. One had it he was mourning in a cave he shared with a hibernating bear whose fur he snuggled against during the cold nights. Another postulated his ripped clothing was the result of a battle with wolves. A third, popular, story, placed him drowning in vodka in a series of taverns frequented by Gentile roughnecks. The latter had some basis in fact.

The cave he slept in sheltered no bear, and the pair of wolves he encountered fled after he hurled a branch at them, screaming rage into the wintry air.

At age twelve, then, Sara stepped into the role of cook, housekeeper and overseer of Aron. She had helped her mother with those tasks and they weren't difficult for her; there was ample time yet to live as a child, socialize with friends and relatives, stroll about, daydream, ponder the lives of creatures in a favorite pond.

Sorrow cast shadows over the family for long dreary months.

It was hard to carry on without Esther's warm presence, her chatter, her influence on every aspect of their lives, and barely endurable for Aron, who would burst into tears, pining for his mother. Daniel and Sara did their best to console him while feeling desolate themselves. The rabbi came by with condolences, prayers for the dead, and read a portion of Ecclesiastes concerning time and the changing seasons, glossing over the sage's observation that life can seem unfair, harsh, and pointless.

They got by, the ache of mourning diminished, winter gave way to spring, and a wonder monk and his dog moved in with them.

The first wonder was performed by his Malamute, Xeno. The monk, Georgi, had broken a leg while tumbling down a steep mountain pass and the dog had saved him from hunger and shock by stealing rabbits out of Daniel's traps. The raw bloody meat was disgusting but meant survival.

When Daniel discovered the raided traps he followed a trail of paw prints and blood drops to the injured monk.

"Praise the Lord!" Georgi shouted.

"Praise your dog," said Daniel.

The swelling was bad but the bone hadn't pierced the skin. Daniel secured the leg with a splint of bark, fashioned a sled out of branches and twine and dragged Georgi back to Kletki behind his mare.

There was immediate consternation in the village about giving shelter to a goy. How would a Christian affect the quality of life in a settlement where the laws of Moses set the standard for faith, reason and behavior? Might such a man be placed there as a test? He could be a thief, a maniac, he could pollute the minds of impressionable young men with stories of the false messiah. It was possible some young women would find him appealing and be vulnerable to seduction. Would his mere presence be unholy and weaken bonds of community forged by centuries of tradition?

Reb Levitsky, well regarded for his shrewd grasp of complicated situations, pointed out the man couldn't move. What could they do?

It was settled. They could do nothing.

Georgi, originally from Kiev, had traveled as far north as Moscow and as far south as Istanbul. He had studied under a variety of mystical sages and visited hallowed shrines. During the seven years since his initiation into the Brotherhood of Creation, an outlawed splinter of the Orthodox Church, he had observed long periods of silence, celibacy, and meditation, and studied texts in five languages. As he went from place to place he earned his keep working at menial jobs, teaching about foreign lands, expounding on the mysteries of gospel, and curing nervousness. It was this last talent that earned him a reputation as a wonder monk. Many families had members who were not exactly crazy but not exactly sane, either. Sometimes entire families fit that description.

To cure nervousness, Georgi used the method of the soothing gaze. He seated the friend—his term for the patient—in a quiet place where they remained silent. Georgi's instructions had been to meet his eyes continually, no matter how difficult that might be, and let his feelings surface. Invariably, the friend would struggle to suppress his feelings and shifted his eyes about. Georgi would continue to gaze peacefully, and eventually the friend would drop his guard, showing expressions of fear, anger, sorrow, loneliness, pleading. Often, he would weep. Within an hour, the friend's face was relaxed and harmonious and his eyes sparkled. When Georgi broke the silence he assured the friend that if he passed this gift on to others his cure would become permanent, and he advised him not to worry if there were occasional setbacks.

Afternoons, Daniel or Sara supported Georgi as he limped to the garden for sun healing. This became the children's hallowed time of day. Out of Georgi's imagination came stories of goblins and trolls, bewitched children, talking animals, underground worlds, musical oceans. Neighboring children were invited to sit and listen and soon, nearly every child in the village was sitting cross-legged and wide-eyed in Daniel's garden. The exception was Eli Kreskin, an unlucky lad who was designated the village idiot. He was the only child of the widow Anna, whose torah-studying husband had died of cholera two years before, leaving her bitter, poor, and very beautiful.

Eli had a thick tongue but no mental impairment beyond a constant sense of shame and loneliness. When he spoke, the words came out garbled and unsymmetrical, as though he were speaking with sawdust in his mouth. Years of painful struggle to express himself and the attendant ridicule had brought him to an impasse. At age nine he was going on ninety, doing a feeble dance with the world around him.

Anna had eavesdropped on one of Georgi's storytelling sessions, observed the spellbound children, and decided that was where her son should be. He wouldn't have to talk, no one would pay attention to him, he might be happy for a while.

She insisted over his protests, leading him a short distance into the garden. "Sit under that tree. I'm sure you'll enjoy it. When it's over you can slip away if you want."

Eyes lowered, he walked to the tree and sat. He saw that none of the children was looking his way, and relaxed. Georgi had observed this business with interest. When the boy glanced at him, he smiled and waved.

The first story that came to mind was of a wandering monk who broke a leg, met a beautiful woman—a vision of Aphrodite—with a troubled son. The monk fell in love with her, they became a family and thrived ever after. Rather, he told of an enchanted forest in Livonia that broke into frenetic dancing on stormy nights when there was thunder and lightning. You could see with each flash of lightning, the trees cavorting in a circle, joined by the wolves, the deer, the hares. The rocks bounced crazily, the very bugs on the ground leapt about in joyful abandon. The swirling wind played a music of lutes and pipes and the pounding rain rendered the sound of drums. When the storm subsided, the forest returned to normal and there was nothing to show that the mysterious frenzy had really happened; but if you put an ear to the ground and listened carefully, you could hear the tree roots and the ferns and the rocks, and the insects, murmuring about what a fine revelry it had been.

Georgi and Anna entered each other's dreams that night as lovers and awoke with poignant craving, sensing one another as a rapture, a glow in the chest.

Georgi confided to Daniel, "I'm more alive, closer to the true mystery of life than I've ever been. This woman is all I need to know of immortality."

Anna plucked a flower from the window box, sniffed it, held it against her cheek, sat on the doorstep staring, as in a trance.

Eli became a regular at the story sessions. Georgi gave him the task of exercising Xeno in the afternoons and serving as messenger to Anna, to whom he tied cryptical, sentimental messages around the dog's neck, such as "Dark eyes take me to Paradise," or "Thinking of an exquisite form," or "The earth sighs where she walks."

Anna, who couldn't read, prevailed on her cousin Simon to decipher the words and in reply she would tie a geranium on Xeno for the return trip. When he was able to walk without a crutch, Georgi hobbled to the widow's house on pretext of looking for his dog, who he knew was with Eli and some other boys, fishing in the river.

"No, I haven't seen your dog." She blushed. "You must be tired, walking like that.

Sit. Let me give you some soup."

"The truth is, I've come to visit," he said. "I've been wondering if you're real or a character from my imagination."

"You've been good for Eli."

"Thank you."

There was a brief silence while they searched each other's eyes as if to decide what to do next. Georgi stroked her hair and was emboldened by her acquiescence to kiss her neck. She moaned softly, said "yes," and led him to her bed.

Rabbi Kline and his court had this problem to grapple with: The widow Anna Kreskin wished to marry the new-comer Georgi Orlov. If she were to marry this man and he persuaded her to christen their children, there would be an intolerable rift in Kletki's way of life.

"The man is already quite popular, and his influence can be seen," said the rabbi. "We must conclude that such a mar-riage would threaten our stability."

They voted unanimously to deny permission for the marriage.

Georgi and Anna continued their companionship with-out bothering to be circumspect while the villagers savored the scandal and chatted about it incessantly.

The popular drift of gossip characterized Anna as a li-centious, lawless woman who was dishonoring the commu-nity and the memory of her husband. Few of the women deigned to speak to her anymore. Leah, a fascinated, though high-minded, neighbor, served as observer and reporter, keeping track of Georgi's comings and goings, and passed on such tidbits as his skill with tools, his lean musculature when shirtless, his propensity to sing ballads in some for-eign language. One shadowy evening she watched him grab Anna and wrestle with her and she heard their laughter shower the air like confetti.

A group of women who may have mixed envy with moral

umbrage agreed to urge their husbands to petition the court for a decree of banishment on the grounds that unlawful and sinful relations were taking place. This gave the rabbi a headache. After all, the village was on Polish soil. How could they exile somebody without official permission? And why would the Polish government approve such a thing, banishment of a gentile and a Jew from some obscure piece of land? And if they were to banish only

Anna, what would happen to her?

He decided to hold a hearing so that all opinions could be fairly considered. Reb Davidowitz protested that such a hearing had never before been held.

"So now we'll hold it."

It was decided a hearing meant men could speak and hear while women could hear but not speak.

On the appointed night, the ninety-five adults who were not senile or ill gathered into the building that served as synagogue and shul. The rabbi and his court were seated in a semicircle facing the audience.

Rabbi Kline explained the purpose of the gathering and asked if anyone had something to say.

"Yes, I have."

Daniel stepped forward. He was a powerful-looking man with wide shoulders, long arms, thick hands. When he gestured, his jacket stretched tightly across his back as though it might rip.

"I want to testify about Georgi Orlov's character. I've known him for two and a half months and I can tell you he's an honest man and a good worker and friendly toward everyone. In my opinion, he would be a good husband to Anna Kreskin and a good father to her son."

Shmuel Rivnik, a tailor, jumped to his feet after Daniel finished.

"Honest? Good worker? Friendly? What is the point here? What are we talking about?"

"Let me remind you of what we are talking about," the rabbi said patiently. "We are having a meeting so that all views may be heard, before this court decides on such a grave matter as guilt and banishment."

Prodded by his wife, Itzhak Frydik rose reluctantly to his feet. "What are the penalties for fornication?" he asked.

The rabbi replied there were various penalties if it could be proven.

Anna's Uncle Saul rose, pointed at Itzhak and yelled, "Shut up, you donkey! You know nothing!"

"This is a hearing and a saying. I can say what I want."

Saul pushed him, Itzhak pushed back, and shortly they were wrestling on the floor. "Stop that fight!" the rabbi shouted.

Daniel and two others subdued them and dragged them out the door.

"If there are any more violent outbreaks, this meeting will be cancelled," said the rabbi angrily. "Before we continue we will sit quietly for a short period. We will then proceed in a respectful, orderly fashion."

It was an interesting quiet, as quiets go. There was at first only the droning buzz of flies. Then a belch, followed by some coughing. A few whispers were heard, some quiet muttering. The muttering gradually increased in volume and intensity until the rabbi slammed his fist on the table. It returned to quiet and the buzzing of flies.

Anna, shamed by all the staring, kept her eyes down or focused on the speakers. When she glanced toward the women, their eyes seemed to gleam like night-shining cat's eyes. She was seated on a bench near the front of the room by the aisle that separated the sexes, in accordance with propriety. She wished Sara could have been present and near. Anna felt her to be a kindred spirit though the girl was only thirteen.

"Now then, who else would add his voice to this hearing?" The rabbi scanned the room. Eventually the blacksmith Herzl rose slowly, stroked his beard and cleared his throat, as a preface.

"Here is the situation as I see it. Our laws forbid intermarriage with people outside our faith. Our laws forbid adultery, whether with people inside or outside of our faith. If we simply follow our laws, then we must tell Anna and her friend to either give up what they are doing, or leave this village."

This was acknowledged with a murmur of approval throughout the room. When it simmered down, the rabbi asked if there were any more views to be expressed.

Georgi got up and approached the judges.

"It is not my desire to disgrace this village or this woman, or myself, for that matter. I want to convert to Judaism and marry Anna. I know Yiddish and I've studied scripture thoroughly. I can seek the Lord in that form as well as any other."

He returned to his seat in the midst of a baffled silence.

"How do we know he's sincere?" someone called out. "Are you sincere?" the rabbi asked.

"Yes."

"Are you willing to be circumcised?"

He replied that he was willing. In truth, the thought of having his foreskin snipped off petrified him.

"This hearing has ended," the rabbi said. "The day after sabbath, the inner circle will decide on the request of Georgi Orlov to convert to our faith and marry the widow Anna Kreskin."

In the first year of marriage a boy was born prematurely, lingered several days and died. The baby, with deep blue eyes set in a wizened face, rarely cried or whimpered but made gentle punctuated sounds, as though expressing wonder. During his brief life he was agonized over, tended vigilantly by his parents and cared for by Sara when they lapsed into exhausted sleep. Each in turn held him, rocked, hummed, strove to infuse him with their strength. Rabbi Kline joined the vigil on the final night, davening, reciting prayers, imploring the Lord's mercy to no avail.

Why did his spirit flicker out like the flame of a candle? The rabbi surmised he may have been an ancient soul appearing in this world for a reason beyond their comprehension—a notion of little comfort to the grieving parents.

Daniel carved an elaborate casket for the funeral and etched onto it, The Lord is my Shepherd, at Georgi's behest.

The baby had been named Peter, after Georgi's father. Eli

inscribed the name with eloquent letters on a slat of wood that Anna set on the mantle.

One child with a speech aberration, another too weak to live. In her grief, Anna blamed herself, wondering if she'd been cursed for some wrongdoing.

The following year she gave birth to a healthy daughter they named Sofi. Dark-eyed like her mother, blonde like Georgi, she made it clear she was going to thrive. She fed easily, slept soundly and responded to the world about her with melodious gibberish.

Family and community had their charm for Georgi, but he found it necessary to get away from time to time. After years as a wandering mendicant he had trouble abiding in sameness. The daily routine of working in Saul's furniture shop and returning always to the same house brought a sense of stagnation, a frustrating cleavage between spirit and the world. Two days a month, he camped in the countryside and meditated, striving to recover the person he had been. Anna tolerated his excursions silently, out of a fear bickering would prompt him to leave one day and never return.

The retreats tapered off and eventually ended as he began spending time in the company of Rabbi Kline, who intrigued him with his willingness to explore realms of thought beyond the ordinary.

"What is revealed in engaging with the complexity of Torah is something greater than words."

"I have a sense of what you mean," Georgi said. "My rejection of churchly authority led me to join the Brotherhood of Creation, but you know, it didn't make much difference. I never did arrive at any special understanding, and was probably afflicted with spiritual vanity, a dramatic notion of myself as a noble seeker."

These talks took place while contemplating moves on the chessboard. Georgi had taught the game to the rabbi, who proved to be a formidable opponent.

"You are still imagining God as something that can be experienced as an entity. That is your dilemma," said the rabbi.

"What, then? Any suggestions?"

"When you realize the mind is no more than an instrument to fix on mundane matters you can grasp, you will move on."

The rabbi's sad features gave way to joy when he spoke this way, like the face of one who sees a beloved friend after a long absence.

"Do you want a task?"

"A task? Yes, certainly."

"Well then, I'm going to assign a brief passage of Torah each week, that you must concentrate on with all your might."

"Which will be first?

"This, from Genesis: 'What have you done? It's the terrifying voice Cain hears after he slays his brother."

"What have you done?" Georgi called to the howling wind, as he walked home to his family.

Reb Jonah Zvi, who considered himself the rabbi's protege and his likely successor, was smoldering. If his jealousy were any hotter it would have consumed him and left but an ash.

He avoided Georgi for fear of striking him dead and spitting on his corpse. How could he presume to get close to Rabbi Kline, this turncoat Christian, this seducer of widows, this goyisher scum? Already, the rabbi was instructing the man in higher concentration, a level reserved for gifted scholars of long standing. Perhaps the white-bearded old man was getting feeble in the head, an easy mark for ecclesiastical swindlers.

It was evident to Jonah's wife Tili that her husband had become quite askew. He flamed into rages over trivial frustrations and stewed over imagined wrongs. He wolfed down his food, and waved off the children when they clamored for attention and play. At his desk, he stared morosely at the wall, neglecting his accounting work and the study of scripture. Most grievously, he lost interest in dallying with her in bed; they hadn't embraced in three weeks. When she sidled up, he shrugged her off and turned to the wall.

The rabbi perceived what was troubling Jonah as did Georgi, and it was evident to Tili, after some deft questions.

Jonah's discourse with Georgi was restricted to monosyllables and hostile stares. When he was forced to occupy a space next to him in the shul, Jonah proceeded as though Georgi himself wasn't present, only the spectre of an obnoxious apparition.

Georgi continued to meet with Rabbi Kline for chess and conversations about everything under the sun. He reminded Georgi of his father Peter who he had last seen when he was twelve years old. Peter had been found in a ditch, beaten to death.

The rabbi assigned Georgi to teach and explore Genesis and the Tree of Knowledge with a group of adolescents that met weekly. With this, Jonah's rage escalated and his depression darkened. He knew then that the Rabbi was persecuting him intentionally, holding that blonde lout of a convert over his head as a goad. But why? What had he done? His self-torment rumbled in this way until it had the momentum of a boulder rolling into Hell. In the realm of madness he found clarity and purpose. He would kill Georgi Orlov and free Kletki from the man's evil spell.

As Jonah walked to the door with a hatchet slung over his shoulder, Tili was seized with terror. She shrieked, clung to him, begged him to stay. He cursed her, struck her, threw her against the wall, and she slid to the floor stunned, staring numbly.

Jonah, trodding his way along a wooded path, guided by a full moon, was calm and peaceful. He knew what had to be done.

He was not very competent at it. Georgi heard him following, trampling branches like a bull, panting heavily, trailing too closely. He stumbled twice and cursed aloud.

Georgi stood in view at a small clearing and waited until the sound of rapid, crunching footsteps drew near. As Jonah approached, Georgi stepped back and shoved him off balance. Bracing himself on the ground, Jonah dropped the hatchet and Georgi pitched it into the woods. Jonah rose halfway up and tackled Georgi. He was the smaller of them, but powerful in his madness. They wrestled for what seemed like eternity, a ball of human struggle gasping for breath. Georgi eventually got Jonah into a neckhold and held steadily as Jonah flailed and wheezed deprecations.

"Goy bastard, liar, fake, I despise you. I'll kill you."

Jonah's energy fizzled out, finally. He slackened, and Georgi let go.

"I don't want to hurt you," he said. "I want to be your friend."

Jonah lay a while, catching his breath. He sat up and rested his head on his knees, crying, at first in loud sobs, then softly. He wept until there were no more tears.

"I'm sorry," he said.

"It's all right, it's finished," said Georgi. " Let's go home."

A storm was gathering, rustling leaves in the trees as they returned to Kletki.

Count Ozo Stefanek admired his reflection in the full-length copper mirror every night before he went to bed. He was infatuated with his broad shoulders, his hairy chest, his thick penis. He flexed in a variety of poses, even straining to see himself from behind.

He particularly enjoyed a view of his rippling back. He practiced arrogant, commanding facial expressions, experimented with lowered eyebrows, sucked-in cheeks, flared nostrils. When his dark narrow eyes glared back at him malevolently he thought such a person might frighten him if he didn't know it was himself.

Sometimes he watched himself get aroused and masturbated, the sperm arcing onto the mirror and dripping down his image. If he was socially inclined, he sent for one or two of the maids for some salacious playtime and the opportunity to bring a new Stefanek into the world. There must have been some thirty of the bastards already sprinkled around the countryside.

The Countess Trina was content to be left out of it. She considered her connubial obligation completed and busied herself with church matters, overseeing the servants, raising the children. Her bedroom was separated from the count's by a long hallway.

Count Stefanek was lord of five square miles that nourished wheat, cattle, horses, fowl, assorted vegetables and fruits, a forest, his peasants, and his own family. A thin tributary of the Vistula ran through it, teeming with so many water creatures it was called Zupna Rybna, "fish soup."

The count and the noblemen of three neighboring domains were in cahoots, forming an army to retrieve a strip of land Hungary had taken thirty years before. The strip, about fifteen miles long, bordering the northeast of Moldavia, had changed hands so many times that so one was sure who had the original claim to it.

The lords, young, energetic and restless, were eager for an adventure that would test their valor and glorify their country.

King Kazimierz was favorable to the plan, reasoning that such a minor conflict, the resurgence of a centuries-old game of snatch and grab, would serve as a pressure release for recent diplomatic difficulties. Better a small fracas with Hungary over nothing, than a costly full-scale war.

King Kazimierz and Ozo had been friends since childhood. Court tutors had instructed them in the disciplines of weaponry, tactics, regency, history, and the responsibilities of leadership. It was on a dare from the then-prince that Ozo pressured one of the more beauteous ladies-in-waiting to remove her clothes, dance for them, allow them to examine and touch her parts and—golden moment!—enter her pudenda. This lady graciously acquiesced to more such lessons until the young hotbloods were ready to explore new fields.

The king was willing to help finance the campaign, but secretly. He stipulated it must appear to be the unique brainstorm of the four noblemen, and not an official undertaking of the crown. A few unruly aristocrats seeking dubious retribution were not to be considered his responsibility. He expected the court of Hungary would be as unwilling as himself to escalate an impromptu escapade into a major conflict, and of course, the Hungarians would inevitably return to wrest back the meaningless strip of land if it was snatched away.

Each count had agreed to form a regiment of three hundred and thirty men from their peasants, their castle guard, and from surrounding villages, a sweeping conscription that would include the hapless males of Kletki.

On the Sabbath, an announcement was posted outside the synagogue saying the village was obligated to furnish sixty men between the ages of fifteen and fifty-five for a temporary draft in defense of the homeland, with dire consequences if the quota was not met. The notice, stamped with the lordly seal of Count Ozo Stefanek, said the men were to be marched off in ten days.

The regional deputy of the Interior Ministry had been informed by his superior in Krakow that he was not to interfere.

Itzhak, fluent in Polish script, read the notice aloud and explained it to those who had gathered after services. The gist of their exclamations of shock and disbelief was, "Why us? God help us !"

Kletki didn't have many more than sixty men who could qualify as soldiers, and of them, none yearned for the military, but what choice did they have? If the eligible men evaded the call, the entire village would be vulnerable to reprisal, perhaps death.

"We've lived peacefully and free of harassment for forty years, now," said the rabbi. "Our peace will have to be suspended for a while."

A tally showed sixty-three men who were of the stipulated age, and were healthy enough to swell the count's ranks and participate in acts of glory. Their names would be inscribed on wood chips, put into a bucket, and the three whose names were drawn would not have to go.

Herman Litvak, the sixteen-year-old son of Meyer, didn't have to go. Reb Davidowitz didn't have to go. Daniel didn't have to go.

The next ten days were spent preparing the young and old who remained, to carry on the necessary work of maintaining a village. Rabbi Kline himself was going to hitch a team and make the weekly trip to the market with whatever they had to sell.

The men who were going had trouble sleeping and when they slept they had bad dreams.

Reb Zekiel Orwitz was in a state of terror as his imagination escalated and spawned images of Hungarians impaling him, hacking off his limbs, setting him on fire. He vomited his food, lost weight, trembled, developed dark wattles under his eyes. At forty-nine, he was nearsighted, flatfooted, and slack of muscle, yet still enough of a man to join a rank and stagger in petrified confusion through a battle.

Upon hearing his dirge and witnessing his deterioration, Daniel brought him to Georgi for a nerve cure. Georgi sat him down, bade him to relax, and gazed at him patiently.

Within an hour, Zekiel nodded off and slumbered peacefully throughout the night. In the morning, well rested and clear minded, he put some belongings into a sack, mounted a horse and left Kletki forever.

A second drawing turned up Daniel's name as the replacement for Zekiel. "Remind me not to help people anymore," he lamented. He and Georgi burst into laughter.

"Ah well," said Daniel, "as long as there's vodka, you and I, we'll get through this war all right."

Count Ozo Stefanek rode his white stallion at the head of his palace guard to see what the village had offered him. Standing about with sacks of food and clothing, they looked no better or worse than the rest of the rabble conscripts he had gathered. Their faces showed similar expressions of bewilderment and they squinted uneasily in the same way. As elsewhere, many of the women were weeping and casting imploring glances at him. He noted that several were very pretty, particularly the young blonde one standing beside the burly man with a sandy beard—apparently her father.

"You there, what's your name?"

" My name is Daniel Brodky."

"I recognize you, you're the hunting guide. You are now Sergeant Brodky and you are in charge of this group. You'll answer to my guard captain. Give him a list of your names and he'll tell you what to do."

Daniel nodded, and asked, "Would you tell us where we're going and how long it may take?"

The count glanced at Sara, who averted her eyes and turned away shyly. "Like fresh wheat," he murmured.

He turned his horse to face the assembly.

"You men are part of a new army formed to take back a portion of land south of here that was stolen from our great nation by the imperialist Hungarians. If we don't fight for what is ours, the Hungarian greed will know no bounds. We must prevent them from coming to our doorsteps. This campaign should be very short because we are depending on the element of surprise. After we have achieved our goal, every man will be given a gold zloty and allowed to return home."

A flurry of murmurs swept through the crowd and faces showed relief. Perhaps it wouldn't be so bad.

They were given helmets, thick leather vests, weapons, and trained to assault foes they didn't know or hate.

The recruits learned to impale bales of hay with pikes, slice boards and branches with swords, stab at one another with scabbarded knives and trade kicks and punches in hand to hand combat. They were taught to advance and destroy, hold a position and fall back, if need be. Their enthusiasm for such stuff was wan in the beginning, so that their cadre saw no recourse but to spur their motivation with ridicule, screams, slaps, kicks, and the flinging of muddy water into their faces.

Gradually, they took on the shape of soldiers, and those shapes of soldiers took on the shape of an army. There was a battalion of archers, two companies of cavalry, a squad to drag a catapult on creaky wheels, a service unit to cook meals and transport supplies, and the remainder comprised the traditional ranks of infantry.

The nobles moved toy soldiers about on a map table, plotted strategies, argued, drank vodka, and generally had a good time.

After a month, the soldiers' families were allowed to visit for a day and a night. The encampment resembled a vast colorful fair, banners waving in the breeze, horse carts, picnics, children running about. At night, streams of smoke and sparks from bonfires rose toward the starry sky in accompaniment to singing and dancing. Under some blankets, husbands and wives caught up on interrupted pleasures of the flesh.

Georgi led Anna away from the revelry to a cemetery where they were sure to have privacy and they made love ardently on grass behind the marble statue of an angel. At sunrise, they awoke near a tombstone inscribed, "Ida, beloved of Boris." One more time then, in memory of Ida and Boris.

At noon, dust raised by families returning to their farms and villages raised a brownish cloud that settled on the river and was swirled downstream.

Friction rooted in intolerance of those who were different led to quarreling and division among the troops. Peasants from southern estates derided their northern counterparts, dubbing them cabbageheads. Northerners responded the southerners were Magyar bastards, implying patrimony from Hungarian rape. Further lines were drawn between villagers and country dwellers, field workers and castle workers, and inevitably, Jews and Gentiles. Along with Kletki, two other shtetls had been tapped for manpower, so that there were some 200 Jews in the ranks, about a fifth of the whole. Among those also, there was friction.

To allay the sporadic brawling, an order was issued proclaiming that fighting among troops would be punishable by public flogging. A Jew from a central village and a Gentile peasant from a local farm were horsewhipped before their peers after having already beat one another senseless. Things calmed down after that, save for occasional skirmishes over theft.

Daniel was given permission from the count to keep his people intact as a separate platoon, which turned out to be less than a blessing; they were assigned to be the reconnaissance unit, tasked with gathering information and relaying it back to the advancing army. If discovered, they were likely to face torture and death.

Meanwhile, they found it pleasant to be apart from the regiment and on their own.

Their officer was Lieutenant Novak, a straw-haired fellow who seemed a bit daft because he was wall-eyed and smiled much of the time. Evenings, he strummed his lyre and hummed odd tunes of his own making. During drill and maneuvers, he showed himself to be an intelligent and capable leader, wisely relaying orders through Daniel, who had good rapport with the men.

The march began on a balmy June morning well after the light of dawn that had been the scheduled starting time. The officers found it maddening to get an army fed, rolled up and ready to go. It required an extra two hours of cursing and shouting orders. A cart had a broken axle, a horse's open sore had to be tended, food and blankets were missing, a cook was bitten by an adder and twenty men had deserted during the night, which accounted for the missing supplies.

The Ferrets, as the Kletki platoon had been dubbed, were ordered to set forth an hour before the main body and maintain a gap of two miles. They were to send a messenger whenever there was anything significant to report.

They moved in triangular formation through cover of forestland adjacent to the road, with Georgi, Daniel and

Novak revolving as point men.

First day out, the Ferrets had nothing more to report than "All clear." Day two, Novak sent Herzl to report that rain had flooded a section of road, and a work crew was dispatched to fell trees and bridge the washout. Day three, the army was poised for action, awaiting word from the Ferrets on the size and armament of the enemy, and its exact location.

Novak, walking at point, was the first to see them, about thirty Hungarian soldiers manning an outpost on a hill overlooking a valley. They moved about among a barracks building, a corral, a storage shed, and what appeared to be a headquarters office.

Novak signaled the men to take cover and be silent, and crawled to a ridge for a better look. Some of the Hungarians were digging a large hole, probably for a new latrine, others were grooming horses. They were obviously unaware of a force of armed men advancing on them with malicious intent. Novak motioned for Daniel and Georgi to come have a look.

"It would be easy," said Novak, "to do it ourselves: Wait until they're sleeping, turn the horses loose, burn the barracks and rout them while they're running around with their pants off."

"That would make us heroes," said Daniel, " but it would cheat our generals out of a victory. I don't think they would like that."

"You're right," said Novak. "We'd better let them play soldier." He sent a runner back to the staging area with the news.

Georgi had a unique variation in mind, and volunteered

to sneak up the hill for a closer look. Novak considered it, dubiously.

"I think we know what's up there, but you can go ahead, if you want. Just don't get caught."

In the dim light of evening, Georgi made his way up the hill slowly, camouflaged by a ridge of bushes. When the outpost was in sight, he removed his helmet, vest and sword, set them under a tree and covered them with leaves. He ended the climb with his arms raised over his head, approached a sentry, and asked in passable Magyar to be taken to the post commander.

Captain Zador slapped a mosquito and flicked it off his arm onto the floor. He was bare from the waist up, pot bellied, had grey hairs on his chest. His face had the droll expression of one who has seen much of life and finds it absurd.

"These mosquitos, if they could drink without itching me, I'd let them have all they like, I don't need so much blood."

His clear blue eyes rested on Georgi.

"I haven't seen you before. Where are you from, and what do you want?"

"I've come to warn you this outpost will be attacked, some time in the morning. A Polish regiment is camped three miles from here, preparing to march."

Zador lowered his feet, sat up straight, and studied his visitor. It was his impression the man was without guile.

"How do you know this?"

"I'm part of that army. I'm with a reconnaissance group

that found you here."

"I don't know if you're a traitor or a liar, or both," said Zador. "Why have you come here?"

"I'm neither of those. Warfare is a cruel and stupid pre-occupation of fools, and I don't want to see anyone slaughtered. The counts who are our generals want to taste blood. If you don't leave here you will be overrun and killed. It's as simple as that."

"How is it you speak our language so well?"

"I spent a year in a monastery near Buda."

"And you are a Pole? These counts, they forced everybody into their army?"

"Yes a Pole, but originally from Kiev."

Zador had some food and wine brought to Georgi and told him he would be confined and guarded while two scouts under cover of darkness went to verify his story. If they found it true, he would be released. Georgi explained how they could maneuver around the Ferrets without being detected.

Shackled in the weapon room, he watched a spider weave a web between the wall and the shaft of a halberd. The creature spun a strand from its body, swung to another strand, and repeated the process until there was a symmetrical, lethal, design. Georgi watched until his mind was quiet and he drifted into sleep.

The scouts returned within three hours to report the stranger was telling the truth.

There was indeed an army, and it was large.

"You can return to your lines," Zador said. "You're a

strange one, but that's in our favor. We'd have been in trouble in the morning."

After Georgi had merged into the ridge his comrades lost sight of him and they were worried his long absence meant he'd been captured, or worse. Daniel was wondering whether he should take some men and go after him.

Finally, they heard him whistle softly and saw him approach. "Well? What?" asked Daniel.

"Well, I looked around their camp and couldn't see much we didn't already know. One of the soldiers was crossing the enclosure in my direction, so I slipped into the storage shed and hid behind some sacks of grain. He came in and leaned against a wall, playing a flute. Sometimes he stopped playing and just stared into space. I feared he'd be there all night, but he did leave, and here I am."

Near dawn, Novak returned from a meeting at the command post, where he was told to keep his platoon in abeyance until the main body of troops arrived, at which time he would receive further orders.

A summer cloudburst had sweetened the air of the assembly area with an aroma of pine. On the meadow, bullfrogs, crickets and birds broadcast their rapture in impromptu melodies while overhead, thin clouds drifted lazily across the sky.

A trumpet sounded. Count Ozo Stefanek, resplendent in battle dress, stood in his stirrups, raised his sword, and exhorted, "To victory!"

Noisily it began, the clanking of weapons, pounding of hooves, and the creaking of wood and iron wheels.

By noon the Kletki platoon, from its vantage point, could see the regiment approach the base of the hill. The count had sent a message commending them for a job well done, and ordering them to stay put, in reserve. Georgi smiled ironically when he saw that the soldiers' faces showed fear, as though they were going into a real battle.

The companies moved into a battle formation the counts had devised the night before, in the course of heated arguments. First, the archers in two groups wide apart, climbed partway up the hill and let loose volleys of arrows. The catapult was brought forward and loaded with a boulder, causing panic when it flew only midway up the hill and careened wildly down again, toward the yelling, fleeing troops. That weapon was abandoned and infantry was sent straight up the center, with two troops of horsemen moving up the flanks.

The Ferrets watched this spectacle from their elevated vantage point, admiring the picturesque figure of their count regaled in armor, a blue plume on his helmet, a lance tucked under his arm, as he heroically mounted the hill.

"Where are the Hungarians?" Novak murmured, peering at the outpost.

"Well," said Daniel, "they may be grouped in the woods for a suicidal counterattack, or they may have gone for reinforcements, or they might just be running for their lives."

"I would guess the last," said Novak. On reaching the plateau, the soldiers were surprised and relieved at having achieved their objective so easily. They milled about, chatted, and waited for orders as the color bearers planted the flag of Poland and banners of their fiefdoms into the ground.

The nobles dismounted from their horses and conferred, etched pictures on the soil, debated, remounted, and led their cavalry in pursuit.

They returned toward dusk with a stag and two boars they had riddled with arrows.

Gangs of bandits roaming the countryside knew that most of the able men in the vicinity had been taken off to war and they took advantage of it to plunder villages and settlements that were virtually defenseless. Two of the gangs entered Kletki on the same night and got into a fight that left half of them dead or wounded. The survivors of the weakest group fled, leaving the victors to plunder as they would.

Anticipating such attacks, the residents of Kletki had outfitted the community's doors with planks and latches that rendered them hard to penetrate without a battering ram, and luckily, none of the vandals had been clever enough to realize that fire would drive the occupants out. They shoved at the doors and ran against them to no avail, while the terrified residents huddled within.

Anna held her crying baby to her breast and put an arm around Eli as the men pounded on the door, yelling, "Let us in, we won't hurt you! Let us in!"

At Daniel's house Sara and Aron crouched by the fireplace, listening to the pandemonium outside. Sara clutched a fireplace poker and Aron held a sledge, for whatever defense those tools might provide. When the pounding came to their door it lasted only a few moments.

The vandals had found a way into the synagogue after breaking a narrow shutter that was inscribed ornately with Hebrew letters. A skinny boy was boosted through and opened the door for the others.

Rabbi Kline was at a table cradling the torah scroll in his arms, swaying, muttering a prayer. "Please, there is nothing here," he said. "This is a place of worship, a house of God." He continued to hold the scroll and watched the intruders with sad, weary eyes.

One of the bandits smashed a chair on the Rabbi's head, and he slumped forward, blood from the wound forming a pool on the table, and dripping onto the laws of Moses.

They took silver plates, candelabras, a box of coins, the velvet cover from the torah scroll, and the horse tethered behind the synagogue. As they hurried from the village, they also made off with grain, geese, a cow, two nanny goats and a dozen chickens.

In the quiet of dawn, the villagers ventured cautiously outside. Reb Davidowitz, Eli, Aron, Reb Levitsky, and several others dragged the bodies of the slain attackers into the forest, dug a large pit, and buried them. A boy of perhaps fourteen, was not yet dead; his rib cage had been cleaved with an axe and he lay semi-conscious, soaked in blood, grey-faced, emitting moans. Anna shaded his face from the sun, placed a cloth over his wound, murmured some soothing patter, waved the men off when they tried to take him. He died soon, and was dragged away and thrown into the pit with the others.

A coffin was fashioned for the rabbi's body and his remains were lowered into a grave in the village cemetery the next morning as Reb Davidowitz led a recitation of the prayer for the dead.

The state deputy and his wife had slipped away during the fracas and taken refuge within the wall of the count's manor. The next day he and the remaining castle guards searched the countryside and found no trace of the bandits. The deputy brought enough weapons to the village to arm every man and boy strong enough to wield them, and showed them how to use them. Word spread among vandals that Kletki was no longer an easy sack and they came no more.

Captain Zador and his men were glad to reach the safety of the garrison, manned by two hundred soldiers and protected by a wall fourteen feet high. On a clear day the tower lookout could see for miles in every direction.

Colonel Kulyakin sent scouts to confirm Zador's report, and they reported it looked like a thousand men ranged around the valley, the outpost, and in sentinel posts within six miles of the garrison. The colonel sent a courier to Buda with the message they were outnumbered five to one, and what should they do?

In Buda, four generals, a war minister, and the king himself, put their heads together and conceived an answer: DEFEND TO THE LAST MAN.

After reconsideration they decided it would be wasteful

and expensive to sacrifice a battalion for a piece of land that was not particularly useful except as a buffer, and they sent a second message overriding the first: IF ATTACK IMMINENT, WITHDRAW TO KOLOZVAR.

The first order was so depressing Kulyakin and Zador downed a bottle of vodka while reviling the king, his four generals, the war minister, and their ancestors, wives, children, and family pets.

On receipt of the second order, they canceled all curses and toasted the health and longevity of all they had denounced.

The ultimate plan of the chiefs in Buda, with the blessing of the king, was to let the Poles hold the place for a while, then move in with a vaster army and squash them. The eldest general, known for his mordant wit, said the whole business was so tedious and predictable that it bored him, and that for his part, the Poles could keep that land forever and stick it up their asses. The minister of war thought that sounded like sedition, but then, the old fool was probably right; official strategy was often like a slow game of chess played by halfwits.

Garbed like a common soldier, Count Ozo Stefanek went reconnoitering with the Ferrets. He took a turn at point and showed a knack for soldiering, taking advantage of natural cover and finding choice spots for observation. He knew instinctively how to use prominent terrain features as guides to keep the platoon from straying.

First day out, they found nothing more significant than

intermittent piles of horse dung. Lieutenant Novak surmised that following the trail of it could lead them to the Hungarian stronghold.

"That's why I made you an officer," said the count. "Because for sheer brilliance you have no equal."

That got a rousing laugh, except from Novak, who tried not to sulk.

Next day, they came upon six horses tethered near a creek. Their riders and a dozen foot soldiers were having their midday meal, resting, chatting, washing themselves in the stream.

It happened so fast they didn't have time to be afraid. On the count's command, they attacked with raised swords, yelling, running toward the creek.

The Hungarians heard and saw the sudden madness coming toward them and went for their weapons.

It was over in a very short time.

Herzl the baker was killed first, after a Hungarian dagger opened his neck.

Ozo plunged his sword into the stomach of a huge fellow who threw him to the ground, choked him a few moments, and abruptly rolled over dead. The count rose, soaked in the man's blood.

Anna's Uncle Saul fled after he was cut above the eyes. His assailant chased and stabbed again, fracturing a rib. Saul turned in fury and slashed the man's shoulder. Blinded from blood in his eyes, he dropped his sword and ran again, bumped into a tree, and fell unconscious.

Daniel barely stepped out of the way of a lance a

Hungarian was aiming at his chest.

He grabbed the soldier's arm, threw him to the ground and kicked him in the head several times, until the man went limp, his eyes rolling loosely in their sockets.

A pair of Hungarians went after Jonah Zvi in tandem, waving their weapons. Daniel followed, and felled one with a sword blow to the head. The other stabbed Jonah's left arm and keeled over screaming, after Jonah, swinging wildly, slashed his leg and abdomen. Jonah collapsed in pain, gasping, "My God, oh my God!"

Novak charged like a maniac, slashing in every direction. He wounded three Hungarians and went after a fourth, who fled in terror.

In the thick of it, Georgi managed to parry and fend off blows without having to maim or kill anybody until he was tackled by a Hungarian who jabbed at him with a dagger and carved a gash into his cheek. Georgi got a grip on his throat, simultaneously banging his head on a rock and choking him until dead..

"Thou shalt not kill," Georgi whispered. He slapped the Hungarian lightly on the face and shook him, attempting to revive him. "No! Please do not die," he implored, "You must not die."

He was dead.

Georgi removed the soldier's helmet and a mop of blonde hair splashed onto his forehead. He appeared to be no more than sixteen or seventeen years old. Georgi felt shame, as though accused by the lifeless eyes that stared at him. "Forgive me," he said. He closed the boy's eyes and recited a Christian prayer.

He rose, surveyed the brutal scene around him, and yelled, in Polish: "THIS WAR IS OVER!"

A Hungarian soldier rushed at him waving his sword wildly. Georgi pushed him aside and walked into the creek, stopped, and yelled, in Hungarian:

"THIS WAR IS OVER!

He removed his clothes and stood naked in the water, roaring, first in Polish, then Hungarian:

"TRUCE! LAY DOWN YOUR ARMS! THIS WAR IS OVER!"

The startled combatants looked at him incredulously. He repeated his harangue: "LAY DOWN YOUR ARMS! THIS WAR IS OVER!"

The fighters hesitated and separated, looking toward their leaders for guidance. The count and the Hungarian lieutenant glanced at one another in consternation, shrugged, and nodded in agreement. The essence of aggression had faded, one imperative giving way to another.

The count and his counterpart, not to be upstaged by a private, exclaimed, in turn, "WE ARE CALLING A TRUCE. LOOK AFTER THE WOUNDED AND DEAD."

The combatants moved apart.

Georgi sat on the sandy bank, staring into the water.

Colonel Kulyakin had interpreted the skirmish at the creek to be the harbinger of an all-out attack on the garrison, and abandoned the fort, as per his saintly orders from Buda.

Lieutenant Novak, scouting alone, saw them streaming through the gate in a long line of cavalry, foot soldiers and wagons. He admired the orderly procession of banners, flags, and colorful uniforms. It was like one of his childhood fantasies come to life.

The Polish nobles decided to leave a hundred soldiers to occupy the fort, which they had christened Fort Eagle, in honor of their nation's emblem. The rest of the troops were to be decommissioned and sent home, and each was given a gold zloty as promised.

Before they were released from service, the reconnaissance men of Kletki were decorated for valor in the war's only battle. In a ceremony on the parade ground, the count draped beribboned medals around their necks, engraved with the Stefanek coat of arms and the flag of Poland. Novak, now a captain, removed and placed his medal around the neck of the count and saluted, as the attendant army exploded into cheers, whistles and applause.

"Lord," murmured the count, proud and happy under the noon sun, "what a wonderful thing this war has been."

Saul, the wound in his shoulder burning with pain, reeled and fainted, and was carried to the shade and given water.

They were issued a flat wagon with two horses to carry the dead back to Kletki. Coffins containing the bodies of Herzl, Jonah and Meyer were set on the wagon and those who were wounded took turns riding on them.

They were glad to be going home, yet there was a prevailing melancholy as they trod along. The fragility and contradictions of their lives had been impressed upon them more powerfully than they had ever expected, or wanted.

When they arrived at Kletki the sun was at that pause before dawn when roosters set about to make a disturbance.

Daniel had a memory of Esther asking why the roosters did that, and her musical laughter when he answered, "If they weren't so loud, how would the dogs know it was time to bark?"

Reb Levitsky had gone ahead of the others to wake the men's families, and the roused villagers awaited their men with excitement and worry.

There were embraces, tears, exclamations of joy, and sorrowfully, the coffins were removed from the wagon and placed in front of the synagogue. It was a day of mourning and lamentation until dusk, when the coffins were lowered into graves.

With night came reacquaintance of warm bodies, deep sleep, and restless, lonely grief for families of the dead.

Two years passed and the Hungarians made no attempt to retrieve the confiscated strip of land from the Poles, though the crown of Hungary had lodged a vigorous protest with the crown of Poland. King Kazimierz replied that some nobles had acted impetuously without official authorization, and the hullabaloo stagnated in limbo.

Twelve more Polish casualties were added to the fort's saga after a brutally cold winter resulted in incidents of pneumonia. One soldier was killed in a jealousy dispute involving one of the prostitutes who came around, and three others froze to death after getting lost and caught in a blizzard. The surrounding farmers continued to farm, having to pay their tribute now to Poland rather than Hungary.

In Kletki, Reb Davidowitz, after a vote of court members, had formally replaced Elias Kline as rabbi. Reb Levitsky had hoped it would be himself but he had to admit Davidowitz was more learned in Torah, and essentially a decent, patient person.

The village's population had increased by a fifth after it welcomed Jewish refugees from Prussia who had been caught in the middle of warring land barons. Their homes had been sacked and burned, livestock taken, a score of men killed, women raped.

Georgi continued to work with Saul making furniture. He had been named to the rabbi's court, which entitled him to be known as Reb Orlov though he encouraged people to call him Georgi, as before. For his thirty-fifth birthday, Anna had woven him an elegant prayer shawl with embroidered stripes and a satin neckband. He smiled to see that his image, in a pool, reflected a beshawled, skull-capped, pious Jew, the sort of person priests of his childhood had inveighed against contemptuously.

Daniel proposed marriage to a prostitute in far away Gdansk who accepted, though she knew he wouldn't remember a word of it when he became sober.

He'd left a waterfront tavern reeling, and encountered her sitting on a pile of rope on the quay.

"Do you want a woman, mister?"

The ships, the water, the woman and himself were floating agreeably in a forgiving, magical haze of alcohol. A woman, the perfect thing! He used to have a woman and he liked it.

""Yes! A woman!"

"Do you have some money?"

"Money!" He pulled a leather pouch from his jacket and jiggled it. He picked her up and walked a few steps but the ground was moving so dizzily under him they collapsed onto the rope.

"Just follow me, mister." Pulling his coat sleeve, she guided him to a dingy cottage near a shipfitter's agency.

With the enhanced perception of alcohol, he perceived her as the quintessential woman, all beauty, charm and mystery, and when she removed her dress the sight of her nakedness evoked a joy he hadn't felt since before Esther's death.

He pulled her onto the bed.

"Not so rough," she admonished, "I'm not made of leather, you know."

When sunlight glowed through the curtains in the morning he had a vague memory of coming there but not the details. They were entangled, her cheek on his chest, her hair under his chin. The touch and smell of her, the strangeness of being there, aroused him again and he rolled onto her.

Afterwards, he asked her name.

"Wanda. I'm your fiance. You asked me to marry you but I know you forgot."

"Well Wanda, I'm too young for marriage, but I would like to see you again."

During the journey back to Kletki he mulled over two satisfactions: He had sold all his carved bowls, cups and plates at the public market for a good profit and he'd had a fine experience with a pretty woman, albeit a prostitute. He decided he would make the long trip again and spend time with her. After all, she was his fiance.

Eli was a frequent presence at the shul, having been guided into the discipline of scholarship by Rabbi Davidowitz, who saw in the boy a talent for absorbing and understanding matters beyond the normal scope of adolescence. The shul practice of reading scripture aloud had brought a boon of healing. Pronouncing each word carefully had loosened, and brought agility to, the muscles of his thick tongue and he was engaging more often and more easily in ordinary conversations.

His half-sister Sofi was the opposite of what he had been—she was spontaneous, loquacious, interacting freely with the world around her.

The young and not so young males of the village were intrigued by the graceful beauty of Sara. At sixteen she was close to maturity, with graceful, womanly curves and a light of intelligence in her eyes. She knew offers of marriage would be forthcoming from one or more of those men who looked at her appraisingly, as though she were a horse or a cow, and she knew her father would respect her wishes and allow her to decline. But if she declined, what would happen to her? She couldn't just take care of Daniel and Aron until she was grey. But how would it be better to take care of someone else? Her father and Aron were no trouble, they helped with the tasks, and they were good company.

Sometimes she daydreamed she was a man, free to accomplish great and difficult things—explore far away places, compose stirring music, construct a palace, invent wondrous contraptions.

Her aunt Rose had assured the family she'd be like a mother after the death of Esther and in many ways she was, yet Esther's absence had left an unbridgeable gap, a strangeness like riding in a wagon with a wobbly wheel or living in a house with a shattered wall.

A bronze statue depicting Count Ozo Stefanek on horseback accompanied by an intrepid-looking foot soldier had been placed on a pedestal in the village a year after the rout of the Hungarian garrison. Daniel, who had a certain rapport with the count, had been asked by the rabbi and his court to explain to him that the laws of Moses forbade graven images, and request of him that the offending display be removed. The count went into a petulant fury at this, warning Daniel that any man who ever again mentioned removing the statue would be hanged, and his flesh fed to pigs.

A neutral arbitration was rendered by the village pigeons, who studied the sculpture from every angle and decided to coat it with pigeon shit.

Rabbi Lohman, a renowned scholar in the erudite circles of Lublin, was born in Kletki and returned there to die. He was perishing from a liver ailment that had no remedy but death. His physician maintained that a concoction made of ground sorrel and bryony might eventually heal the troubled organ but it worsened, and Rabbi Lohman lost patience with medicine. He named his eldest son to be his successor and bade the youngest—his favorite, though a dunce at Torah—to hitch up the team and deliver him to the place of his birth. The son Joshua found lodging for his father at the house of Meyer the tailor who had been one of the soldiers killed in the infamous battle of the creek.

Meyer's childless widow continued to make overcoats from a tall pile of cloth stacked in a corner as she hummed and talked to herself. She claimed she was talking to the spectre of her departed husband, conferring about patterns, sleeve lengths, buttons, choice of materials, and declared with pride she was replicating his exact work.

Since she was a relatively serene person and a good cook, Rabbi Lohman was content to tolerate her strangeness. And then, who could say? Maybe Meyer's spirit was still lingering, linked to this world through the phenomenon of overcoats. Whatever the case, it was a comfortable place to be, and near enough Lublin for his questionable physician to pay an occasional visit.

Rabbi Lohman had high standing among many but not all torah scholars, derived from his lofty interpretations of scripture. As example, he explained Exodus as a paradigm of the soul's search for freedom from the limited realm of the

senses, He asserted that the inner core, the essential meaning of Exodus, was that we should emulate Moses and leave
Pharoah—the world —behind, and journey beyond the familiar preoccupations of our minds until we arrive at our
own Mount Sinai, the peak where we commune with God.

His commentaries on scripture were generally inspired
by that mystical, allegorical bent and he was widely revered
in metaphysical circles as a genius, perhaps even a prophet,
though within orthodox circles where conventional thinking
was considered a duty and a virtue, his ideas were dismissed
as no more than high-flown conjecture. One traditionalist
denounced him as "An intellectual empire builder, a mental
barbarian who would colonize the Torah with his own self-
serving notions."

Rabbi Lohman sent that man a letter complimenting
him on his deft use of analogy without attempting to refute
him, which aggravated the critic all the more, who felt he
deserved a head-on confrontation.

As his condition worsened and his strength ebbed he
felt a psychic lightness, an ongoing sense of peacefulness.
Evenings, he would sit on the porch, a blanket draped on
him, watching light turn to shadow just as his life was doing,
and surrendering to the natural arrangement of things. He
had done his work in this world and was ready to be released
from a tired, worn-out body.

Sara occasionally passed by on some errand and the
rabbi noticed with pleasure the gentle radiance she exuded.
He thought of a line from the Song of Songs: "Behold, thou
art fair . . . "

He waved to her one evening and asked her to come and sit. "What's your name, child?"

"Sara,"

He looked into her eyes and found it remarkable there could be as much to marvel at in a person's eyes as in the most exalted scripture. Perhaps more.

"What does your father do?"

"He's a woodcarver and a hunter."

"Is he a religious man?"

"I don't know. He might be. He doesn't go to the synagogue very much and he doesn't talk about it, but he has a good heart."

"I see."

It seemed to him the girl's eyes opened to infinity. Gently, he touched her head.

"A son born to you will be a boon to this world, a great servant of the Lord, a bringer of hope. You may go now. I'm tired and I want to sleep."

Sara puzzled over his words as she walked. Why would he say such a thing? She thought of a son, what he might look like, what he might be like.

Home, she stoked the fire in the hearth, hung a kettle over it, put in the makings of a stew—carrots, cabbage, goat meat—and watched it boil. She said aloud, "A son?"

"What did you say?" asked Daniel.

"Nothing."

Daniel continued showing Aron how to carve a bevel on the rim of a serving bowl. "Once you master this, you can do anything."

The next week, Rabbi Lohman died in his sleep. The funeral service was attended by friends, relatives, and admirers from near and far. He was buried next to the grave of Rabbi Kline, who had been a childhood friend.

The count had been out of sorts lately; nothing pleased him and many things displeased him. He struck the countess when she contradicted him about the way to discipline a wayward peasant. Her eye was discolored for ten days. She imagined ways to poison him or have him murdered. He berated the children for trivial infractions he normally would have ignored. In defense, they developed an intracastle warning system that enabled them to dodge out of sight when he was coming. He hotly accused his overseer of distributing more grain to the peasants than had been allotted to them. The count's suspicion had been accurate, though the overseer denied it vehemently. Why not? Didn't the peasants have a right to eat, after the torment of their bones? He slipped away that night with a substantial hoard of coins he had amassed over the years.

The count had a falling out with a neighboring nobleman over whose arrow had pierced the neck of a swimming duck, and whose had merely penetrated its wing. Their argument was close to developing into a duel until Ozo grabbed the duck from the retriever's mouth, threw it into the pond, stuck his dagger into a tree and rode off, leaving his companion to marvel at what a sorehead he was.

In his bedroom that night he studied his face in the mirror, alternating his expressions, a diversion that brought only ennui, the same old face shaping into the same old configurations. Such sameness, it was depressing. Opting for a changed perspective, he darkened the room, placing only a small candle on each side of the long mirror.

Sitting naked and cross-legged, he watched himself impassively. In a short while astonishing things began to happen: His face was transformed into a variety of countenances with a variety of expressions. None were his, yet in a sense they were, springing from some untapped source in his consciousness. It was as though his mind had sprung a leak. In each case, the shadowy outline of his usual face dissolved momentarily into another. None looked particularly happy; the expressions were alternately serious, sorrowful, angry, anxious, lonely. There was a spooky quasi-human quality to them, like the ghoul masks crafted by Janek, the tool maker. The stream of apparitions lasted several minutes until the mirror went blank, bereft of even his own face. Presently a white and gold light glowed on the mirror and formed into the face of a young boy with wide eyes and a mischievous smile, who seemed both impish and compassionate. After a few seconds that face dissolved back into the white-gold light, and disappeared. Ozo's familiar visage stared back at him again.

He lay on the floor watching the stars glimmer through the window. They had never been so bright. Before he fell asleep he thought of the vast spaces between them and wondered if stars could be as lonely as people.

She had removed the bandana the Jewish women usually wore, and her blond hair was flowing over her shoulders and down her back. The count recognized Sara right away, and recalled she was Daniel's daughter. Of the women of Kletki, she had made the most vivid impression on him. He watched her pick blackberries from the tangled vines near the edge of the stream.

He dismounted, tied the rein to a sapling, patted the palomino gently, put a finger to his lips and made a shush sound. Quietly, he walked further down the hill for a better look.

She removed the shawl that covered her blouse and he saw that her arms were lithe and somewhat tanned from the sun. She pulled the thorny vines apart gingerly with one hand, picked berries with the other and dropped them into a basket that also contained wildflowers. A few berries went into her mouth instead of the basket, after she blew the dust off them. When she decided she had had enough, she set the basket behind her, cupped her hands and scooped some water into her mouth. She sat on a flat boulder, took off her shoes, raised her skirt to her knees, dipped her feet into the water and plunked pebbles into the stream. Her legs, nicely shaped, were whiter than her arms.

The count pondered how best to approach without frightening her and putting her on guard. He decided to announce himself gently at a safe distance, as you would approach a doe. Nimbly, he made his way down the hill under cover of foliage. When he was within view he called to her.

"Hello. Hello there. It's me, Count Ozo Stefanek."

Her view obstructed by the sun, she saw a large male figure she didn't recognize moving slowly toward her. She removed her feet from the water, straightened her skirt, stood, shaded her eyes with one hand, and saw clearly that it was the count. She'd seen him only once before, but the grandiose statue had emblazoned his image in her mind, indeed in many minds. She restrained an urge to flee, and waited.

"I know you. You're the daughter of Daniel," he said, leaning nonchalantly on a branch he'd used as a walking stick.

Without his battle armor. Wearing simply a tunic and trousers, he didn't look so lordly and menacing. He tipped his hat, smiled, performed a chivalrous bow.

"Are you enjoying this day?"

Sara thought it odd his eyes were narrow and somewhat slanted, like those of the Mongolian trapper who peddled furs throughout the region.

"Yes, thank you."

"It looks like you have enough berries for forty tarts."

"Oh. Please have some."

She offered the basket, he took several and gestured it was enough.

"Sometimes I ride in these woods when I want to get away from my responsibilities," he said. "I pretend I'm nobody in particular and it cheers me up. Which reminds me, I don't know your name."

"Sara."

"Well, Sara, I have a roast pheasant and bread and wine in my saddle bag, and I'd be honored if you'd join me for lunch."

"I think I'd better go home now," she said, "or my father

and brother will wonder what happened to me."

He affected a tragic expression, put his hands to his head and staggered in mock dismay.

"Lunch alone! On a beautiful day! She won't stay.!"

He faced her, smiling, and said, "You must change your mind, really you must. If you don't share my lunch, I'll lie in the water and I will drown myself."

She laughed out of surprise to see the count out of character, clowning. "Well all right," she said, "but I can't stay here much longer."

He brought the saddle bag down, put a cloth on the ground and set the meal on it. "Just take it with your fingers," he said. "We're not fancy here."

He uncorked the wine and offered her the first drink. She winced at the unfamiliar sharp flavor, so different from the ceremonial wine she'd had before, yet it gave her a sense of well-being.

When they were finished they cleansed their hands and mouths from the stream, dried themselves with the cloth and tossed the bones for scavengers to pick clean.

After the food and wine, Sara felt a little drowsy. It didn't seem so urgent anymore to get home.

How had it happened? Had she let him do it, or had he simply done it, without her will mattering? It seemed one moment they were resting in the shade; the next, he was embracing her, kissing her neck, lying on top of her. And then his mouth was pressing on hers and his hands were on her legs, stroking, climbing, fondling her behind and touching her sex. Had she said no? She couldn't remember.

She was shocked to see his organ, large, veined, fleshy, pointed at her. She struggled and he said softly, "No, no, it's all right, it won't hurt you. You'll like it, you'll see."

There was at first pain which made her gasp, and then a feeling of pressure, of her opening being packed, invaded. While he moved, he pulled out her breasts, kissed them, kissed her face. His face was damp with perspiration.

Incongruously, in the midst of feeling pinned down as though by a monster, she watched a cherubic little cloud pass in front of the sun, obscure it, and drift away,

It was strange, his eyes, the way they glowed. They were unguarded now, opened wide, showing flickers of tenderness. When he climaxed, he kept his eyes on hers, curled his brows and made staccato grunts of rapture. He rolled off, placed a hand on her stomach lazily, and stared at the sky.

"That was superb," he said.

She didn't want to utter a sound or move. She wanted to float away to a year ago, or melt into the ground, or disappear into the air.

He felt his mind and body slip into utter lassitude, heard the muted sound of a bee buzzing somewhere in the distance, and drifted off to sleep.

Her skirt was still raised above her navel. She felt some pain and then nothing, and then more twinges of pain, with a sensation of stickiness between her legs. She moved his hand off her stomach, sat up and looked. A small pool of blood had trickled out of her, along with some of his whitish-yellow fluid.

She went to the stream, took off her skirt and sat, letting the cool water cleanse and soothe her. She wished her mother were still alive. She looked at the count sleeping peacefully as a child. She didn't know she was crying until the tears slid down her cheeks and onto her chin.

She dressed, picked up the basket with its blackberries and wildflowers and went home.

At first they saw her moods as a phase, difficult but temporary, and they weren't very concerned, but her aloofness and moping continued until it was obvious something was wrong, her gloom was so far out of character.

She spent a lot of time sitting alone, staring into a void, didn't go to visit anyone, and if friends came by she said she wasn't well, or tolerated them with an air of edginess and abstraction.

Her conversations with Daniel and Aron were brief with none of her characteristic humor and enthusiasm. She took scant interest in anything and performed her household chores dully, mechanically. The usual smile lines around her mouth were turned downward.

After a week of it, Daniel blurted out, "What's wrong with you? Why are you so unhappy?"

She responded as though his concern were a blow, and she felt suddenly attacked, groundless, exposed. She dropped the towel she was holding and wept, aware that her father was looking at her with a mixture of confusion and worry.

"It's nothing," she said. "Really nothing, I'm just in a mood these days."

"What is it?" he demanded. "Why are you crying? What is the matter with you?"

"It's nothing." She ran out of the house into a neighboring orchard, sank to her knees and wept until empty.

Daniel asked Georgi to have Anna talk to Sara to see if she could find out what was troubling her. She and Anna were close, often carried on far-reaching conversations about everything under the sun.

Anna and Xeno found her in the garden, pulling weeds around a patch of squashes.

Xeno jumped on Sara and licked her face, his strength almost knocking her over. Laughing, she shoved him off, and hugged him fondly.

"I haven't laughed for such a long time now," Sara said. "Something happened, and I don't know what to do about it."

"Is it something you can talk about?"

"I don't know. Maybe. But I'm so ashamed of it."

"I'm listening."

After a pause, she began talking, haltingly at first, watching Anna's face for signs of shock or disapproval. Anna sat patiently, letting the tale unravel as Sara was able.

"And so I left him there and walked home," she concluded.

"So it happened," said Anna. "You have nothing to be ashamed of. What could you do? You were trapped. You couldn't make him disappear."

"I don't know if I should tell my father. How could I look at him and tell him a thing like that?"

"I don't know either. That would be hard. Let Georgi tell him. It might be better for everybody."

Daniel had been chopping wood when he heard it. He was stunned into silence for a few moments, before he exploded.

He picked up a log and threw it onto the ground. He picked it up again and hurled it furiously about twenty feet.

"The count did this!"

"The count will pay!"

He sunk an axe into a stump and paced about in agitation.

"Be careful what you do," said Georgi, "or you could put the whole village in danger." Daniel cast an exasperated glance at Georgi.

"The village! He can't hide behind the village! Let me be, now!"

He walked until nightfall, along the river, into the woods, in a tempest of fury and revenge. He eventually calmed down enough to realize he had been more concerned with his rage than with Sara and her suffering. When he got home his anger was under control, smoldering in the dark.

She watched him warily when he came into the house. He saw her fear and felt a stab of grief. He sat beside her, took her hand and said, "I heard. I'm sorry. I'm sorry it's been so hard on you. I promise he'll never bother you again."

She didn't want to cry but tears came, in a flood of relief. At the same time, she wondered what he meant by that last remark.

The count thought of her constantly. He dreamed of her. One night he awoke and reached for a shining blonde spectre next to him. It was an illusion. Or was it?

The countess Trina saw that he went about with an abstracted, smooth, dreamy expression, and that he was kind to the children again. She thought he must be in love and she was jealous even though she hated him, or used to, she was confused. On a black moonless night, she came to his room, took off her gown and slipped into his bed, interrupting his dream with the heat of her skin and the surprise of a body. Wordlessly, they merged into an embrace more erotic than they had known. The lust shimmered, glowed, was mysterious, and they lost track of who they were.

When it was over she went back to her room, washed her body with rose water and watched candle shadows flicker on the wall.

After the inevitable roosters and the dawning light wakened Ozo, an odor of sex in the bed and a memory of the surreal lovemaking aroused him and made him turgid again.

He draped a blanket around himself, walked down the hall to Trina's room and knocked softly.

"It's me, Ozo. Let me in."

She slid the latch, opened the door slightly, and said, "What do you want?"

Her eyebrows raised, she watched him coquettishly, somewhat defiantly. She was still naked.

Without answering, he pushed the door open, picked

her up, lowered her onto his stiff member, and walked to the bed. In daylight the sense of time was more familiar and the quality of sex more personal. When they peaked, the pleasure of it vibrated in their nerves like lute strings.

Satiated, Ozo stopped reminiscing about his encounter with Sara. Every third or fourth night, he and Trina played intriguing games, meeting at the river, the stable, and even the chapel, where, dressed as a priest and a nun, they seduced each other wickedly.

Daniel waited outside the manor for the count to ride alone so that he could follow him and kill him.

On the third day of waiting, the gate opened and Count Ozo Stefanek rode out with the local priest and the bishop from Krakow. They separated at a crossroad, the count reining his steed onto a grassy path.

Daniel whispered, "Go," nudged his horse with his heels, and the horse broke into a trot.

"Hello! Hello Count! It's me, Daniel Brodky." The count squinted curiously.

"The sergeant from Kletki. Welcome. What brings you here?"

"I'm looking for help to kill a bear. It's not far from here. When it came after me I shot an arrow toward it and I got away from there fast. It's big, angry and aggressive. If you could spare a couple of soldiers we might be able to bring it down. It's a holy terror."

"Let's go, then," said the count. "We can do it ourselves. What do we need soldiers for? Show the way."

They followed the path until it led into a thick forest. "Just what this day needed," said Ozo. "An angry bear."

"Well said, Count."

Their plan, when they reached the locale of the hypothetical bear, was to dismount, stalk quietly on foot, riddle their quarry with arrows, and charge boldly with sword and axe. If the bear charged at one of them, the other would sink a blade into it. Despite his resolve to extract vengeance, Daniel's heart was pounding and he was soaked with sweat. He had killed in the so-called war, but murder was something else, a sojourn into nightmare. He reminded himself it was the right thing to do, the brute had it coming. "In there," he whispered. "That's where it happened.."

They dismounted and crawled quietly into a thicket on the edge of the clearing. It's now or never, Daniel decided.

He pulled his axe from its sheath and prepared to strike.

Suddenly a loud noise. He froze in dread, and turned. Preposterously, there was a bear crashing at them through the thicket, huge, roaring, and angry. Behind her, her cub watched in confusion.

They rose quickly to their feet, ran into the clearing, put arrows on their bowstrings and let fly. One arrow lodged in the animal's stomach, the other whizzed past, into the forest. The bear let out a deafening roar of pain, charged at Ozo, slashed his face, and knocked his bow away with a powerful swat across the shoulder. The count screamed in agony.

Daniel moved behind the bear, raised his axe and sank it

cleanly, with all his strength, into the bear's neck. The creature reeled, rolled over, grunted, and died, her eyes fixed on Daniel in a sad stare.

The count was unconscious, his clothing soaked with blood. Daniel saw that the first blow had ripped his eyes, and he would be blind.

"Enough revenge, then."

He dragged Ozo to the shade of a tree, poured water onto his wounds and covered them with webs and nettles to stem the bleeding. He carried blood in his cupped hands from the bear's neck to a nearby mound, hoping it would deflect ants and other pests away from the count.

As he rode off he saw that vultures were not yet circling overhead.

At the manor he explained in a rush, his version of what had happened, and returned to the clearing with the countess, her physician, four soldiers, and a horse-drawn cart.

The count was inert but still breathing as the soldiers lifted his unconscious body onto the cart. After the physician placed a dampened bandana over his mutilated face, Trina ordered the soldiers to leave the bear alone, forbidding them to return to skin her or take her head.

The cub stood by his mother, whimpering. Trina told the guard captain to bring him back to the manor and see that he was fed and taken care of.

Daniel watched them go and rode slowly back to Kletki, leaving the bear to the insects, the wolves, the rats and the buzzards.

Part Two

THE HOLY EMPIRE

In the year 800 A.D. Charlemagne was crowned Emperor of the Holy Roman Empire by Pope Leo III of Rome. He was to be God's temporal ruler, in concord with the pope, who was designated God's spiritual ruler. The empire lasted a thousand more years, until Napoleon rearranged the map of Europe and Francis II relinquished the title of emperor.

Most of the emperors were Germanic, whose positions were weak or strong according to their support from princes and nobles within the empire, and from the pope. Generally, the emperors had prestige and large land holdings, but limited power, though, some who were cunning and bold expanded the empire, ruled with a strong will, and dared to depose popes who wouldn't dance to their tunes.

When Daniel decided to leave Poland in 1459 and cross the empire to Spain, the Holy Roman Emperor was Frederick III, who was struggling with Hungary to keep control of Bohemia and Austria. The Ottoman Empire threatened Hungary, Hungary threatened the Holy Roman Empire and the Holy Roman Empire was losing the momentum to threaten anybody. As always, the political boundaries of Europe were shifting like an amoeba, changing with the fortunes of war. At that time most European states were less secure places for Jews than Poland or Lithuania. During the Plague of Black Death a rumor had got started that Jews caused it by poisoning wells and streams and thousands of Jews were slaughtered. Thousands more Jews were slaughtered when libels spread that they were using the blood of Christian children for foul rituals. When legions of crusaders crossed the empire they routinely massacred Jews where they found them.

Sporadically, someone would charge that Jews were desecrating the Host by contaminating eucharist wafers, and again they would be sought and killed by fervent mobs.

When an occasional compassionate pope ordered an end to the mayhem, he was generally ignored.

Sometimes princes, officials, clergy, or the emperor himself, offered protection against bloodthirsty mobs of Jew haters, and there were intermittent periods when the Jews were left in relative peace. Those periods were interrupted by forced conversions, expulsions, outrageous taxation, and confiscations of property.

With that, a band of travelers from Kletki had to plot how to wend their way through the empire without getting killed, beaten, robbed, raped, and forced into servitude.

"You're leaving Poland?" Wanda asked. "Where are you going?"

Daniel shook the vodka bottle to estimate content, took a final swig and tossed it under the piling. A curious gull swooped over and away.

"Well, I've heard Spain is warm and sunny, has good wine, and Jews have lived there for hundreds of years. They say the wood of the olive tree is fine for carving. It's time to go. We have to go"

"But why do you have to go?"

"My daughter was harmed by a certain count. I settled that matter. In six months, a baby will be born. Sara's been gloomy and she'd be ashamed to give birth in our village of blabbermouths. A new place, a new life, will be better for everybody."

"I want to go too. Take me with you! Please!"

He noted the eager, childlike expression on Wanda's face and laughed. A woman like her? But why not? He lifted her and twirled her playfully.

"To Spain? What would we do with you?"

"I can cook and make clothes. I'm strong and healthy, I will be a good woman for you.

I don't want to live here anymore and do what I do. I've saved plenty of coins."

"Can you learn Spanish?"

"Sí. Will you take me?"

"Sí!"

She thought it best not to let Daniel know what a Spanish sailor had told her, with an attitude of boasting:

That Jews were despised by many Christians in Spain and had been swindled, attacked, forced to convert, and murdered. Perhaps it had gotten better.

The return to Kletki was blessed with pleasant weather except for a rainstorm they evaded at a riverside hostelry where they were the only customers. Logs blazed in the fireplace, a hearty meal was served, and the proprietor's daughter serenaded them on a clay flute. They succumbed to deep sleep in a bed of goose down, waking at dawn to the bray of a donkey announcing that rain had given way to sunshine.

Daniel lay quietly, staring at the wall. Wanda curled into him and sighed contentedly, sharing the silence until it felt strange.

"What are you thinking about?" She guessed what was coming, and waited.

"Well, I'm thinking this: I'm thinking of how many men you must have woken up with on mornings like this, and I'm wondering if I'm any different from them. I'm wondering if you can tell me apart from them and if maybe you liked some of them better."

"I'm going to tell you straight from the heart, Daniel, that I didn't care for any of them. They were strangers to me, faces without souls. I was with them to get money to stay alive, that's all. You're the only man I ever cared for. Ever."

He lapsed back into silence after hearing the words he wanted to hear, though they may not have been strictly true.

Somehow, the word "soul" had had a soothing effect on him.

Wanda sensed the calming.

"I won't bring it up again," he said, aware such thoughts would probably recur until the distractions of time erased them.

The donkey brayed again to herald the obligations of a new day.

Six nights later they returned to Kletki in the light of a waning moon that gave the village a semblance of peace.

Before they entered the house, he whispered, "For the while, until the children get used to you, you'll sleep in my bed and I'll sleep by the fireplace."

He lit candles and woke Sara and Aron, who struggled out of their beds sleepy-eyed, staring curiously at the strange woman.

"This is Wanda, my friend from Gdansk. She's coming to Spain with us."

The hellos gave way to an awkward silence. Daniel exclaimed, "Well!" and pulled gifts from his pack, as he customarily did after a journey. There was a scarf for Sara, a knife for Aron, and some piroshki that had gotten squashed and crumbly from bouncing in the wagon.

The children made appropriate gratitude sounds, glancing appraisingly at Wanda. They had never seen anyone quite like her. She was tall, lean, had ample breasts, copper red hair. Her deep-set brown eyes had a fervid, glowing quality.

"Your father has told me so many things about you, it almost seems like I know you."

Aron couldn't take his eyes off her. At thirteen, women had taken on a new aspect for him that inspired fantasies and a trace of guilt. He was intrigued Daniel had produced such an astonishing woman. He had assumed the trips to Gdansk were confined to selling his carved goods in the market and sleeping. He offered one of the piroshki to Wanda. She broke off a piece and nodded her thanks.

"Are you going to marry my father?"

"Hey!" Daniel roared. "Enough of that. Wanda is our friend, and she's going to live with us like a member of the family. She is a seamstress who worked at making sails for the ships and we met one night on the dock and we talked and we liked each other.

That's all you need to know for now."

"It's all right," said Wanda. "He just wanted to know. We haven't talked about marriage but we're very good friends. I hope we can all be very good friends."

"Welcome to our home, Wanda," said Sara. "I'm going back to bed."

"Yes, good night," said Wanda. She noticed Sara's midriff revealed no sign yet of her forming baby.

They all turned in. It was mid-October and dimly, a church bell in the distance tolled the end of a harvest festival. Daniel had a vision of peasants dancing around bonfires, drinking and carousing, romancing in stacks of hay. A line from a traditional song flitted through his mind: "Poland, sacred mother of us all."

He thought they might miss the place for a while.

Daniel and Georgi and Anna sold their homes at a reasonable price to two of the families that had taken up residence in Kletki after fleeing Prussia. Thus, they broke ties with all that was familiar and set out for the unknown, despite fearful warnings from relatives, friends and neighbors.

After teary goodbyes, they departed in two wagons, each drawn by two horses. In the manner of the people called Gypsies, they had fitted the wagons with sides and roofs to serve as meandering cabins. As protection against violent Jew haters, they had painted crosses on the sides so that they could masquerade as Catholics on a pilgrimage to Rome. That had been Georgi's brainstorm. Daniel, who supposed God didn't care one way or another, had no misgivings about it, though many of the villagers suspected the Lord might smite the deceivers for betrayal.

Rabbi Davidowitz was relieved to see the wagons disappear from view after he had done what he could to deter them, lest God put a hex on the village.

Naomi, an avid gossip, had seen Sara vomiting into a patch of weeds three consecutive mornings and surmised correctly that she was pregnant. Rumors of rape by some passing Christian were a popular explanation for her condition, though other possibilities were not ruled out. Sara was forced to endure accusatory glances and melodramatic hand-wringings until they became only a minor annoyance and she was relieved to discover, finally, that she didn't care, in fact, felt no shame at all. She was glad to be leaving Kletki for adventure in the company of people she loved and trusted.

Before the travelers rounded the curve that would put the village out of sight forever, Daniel halted the wagons, picked up a handful of dust, said farewell, and let go of it.

They ambled toward Silesia at an easy pace, enjoying the temperate mood of autumn with its amber hues.

They walked alongside the wagons when the road was rutted or steep and rode when it was smooth. Occasionally, farmers and townspeople honored their lofty purpose with gifts of food and lodging, and Georgi assured them God would reward their good will. To avoid any sharp questioning that might arouse suspicion, he explained that as devout way-farers, they were obliged to practice pious quietude, which meant speaking politely, with as few words as necessary.

Eli, who dabbled in poetics, made daily entries on a slate in carefully drawn Hebrew letters expressing such senti-ments as, "Like Moses with a promise to keep, we pursue a destiny others will reap." He read it to Wanda who declared it one of the finest things she had ever heard, and implored him to teach her to read and write. He obliged gladly, show-ing her how to form letters into words. Sara and Anna en-treated him to teach them too, and their days on the road were enhanced by the transformation of such sounds as aleph, mem, and tav into understanding.

At Silesia near the town of Oswiecim, they stopped at a large sign picturing a skull.

Written in Polish and German, it said, DEATH PLAGUE HERE. "What now?" asked Georgi. "This is the road we want to be on."

"When we get to the town we'll see how bad things are," said Daniel. "Our best bet is to move through quickly."

Oswiecim was grey and gloomy, mesmerized in a fog mingled with smoke billowing from an iron smelter near the center of town. There were no people in sight, only an orange cat that darted from a doorway, ran between the wagons, and disappeared under a building.

As they approached the smelter, two uniformed men, their lower faces covered with bandanas, ran toward them.

"Halt!" they shouted. "Stop here!"

They blocked the road, their arms raised. "Stop your wagons!"

"What do you want?" asked Georgi. "Who are you?"

"We're officers of the emperor," replied the eldest, "here to see that the dead are burned, to keep the plague from spreading. We need all the supplies you have and we need your wagons to transport the dead."

"How many of you are there?" asked Georgi.

"We have ten soldiers carrying bodies to burn in the smelter and two old men from the town are helping us. The other townspeople have died or fled. More than half of them are dead."

Georgi translated the German to Daniel.

"We'll die ourselves if we touch those bodies," Daniel said. "We'll be doomed like these soldiers. This is no time to be saviors."

"You're right. We have to get out of here."

"Tell them to direct us to the bodies and tell them we'll meet them there," Daniel said, "and when we get there, we'll whip our horses to a run and keep going until this place is behind us."

The bodies, emitting a stench like decaying garbage, were piled on mounds near an abandoned lumber mill. Many were decomposed beyond recognition and others were recently dead.

"All right, enough of this, let's go," Daniel said.

The officers who had halted them turned in from an alley. "Whoa, stop! Where are you going?" one shouted.

"Look, you're crazy to touch those corpses," Georgi said. "They'll make you sick. You don't have to take them to the smelter, just leave them and get out of this town. Save yourselves before it's too late."

The younger officer drew his sword and moved toward Daniel's wagon. "Halt in the name of Emperor Frederick!"

"Never mind," said the elder. "Let them go. He's right. We've already lost eight of our soldiers to plague. We'll burn this accursed place to the ground and be done with it. If we're lucky, we'll get out of here alive."

Several hours later, the travelers camped for the night on a rise to the west of Oswiecim. The night was illumined by a conflagration that spread thick smoke for miles around.

Eli told Aron he could hear the scream of tormented souls as they left this world for the next one.

"Be quiet, that's spooky," Aron said. "I don't want to hear it." They slept fitfully that night, with troubled dreams.

Sara placed her hand over her abdomen and repeated "adonai, adonai," to soothe the child within.

Continuing southwest, they passed through more settlements that had been ravaged by the plague and abandoned, leaving corpses in the wake of fleeing survivors. At the last town, barely inhabited, they had a skirmish with a group of four men who attempted to get onto their wagons. One reached out a bony arm and grabbed Aron, who lost balance and fell to the ground. Daniel kicked the man's head and he and Georgi jumped into the group, punching and shoving until the men backed off, too weak and demoralized to fight back. They fled, except the eldest, who lay on the ground weeping, his emaciated cheeks made grotesque by dirt streaks of tears.

"Please give me some food," he implored. "I'm starving."

Georgi shook his head in dismay after Anna threw an apple to him. "Don't say it," she said. "It's a waste of our scarce food."

"So it is, but I won't say it."

They continued on, worried they may have been contaminated.

The following morning, Aron complained that his head hurt. Wanda put a palm to his forehead and felt the heat of fever. There was a rash on his face and his eyes glittered abnormally brightly. By afternoon, Sofi had also developed a rash, along with pain in her head, eyes and throat. Wanda urged Daniel to stop so that they could tend to the children. "That house down the hill, we'll pull up there," he said.

It was a small farm deserted by humans except for an old woman they buried after finding her dead on a stack of hay behind the barn. It was agreed, at Wanda's insistence, that for general protection, no one but she should nurse the children. She led Aron and Sofi into the farmhouse and bade them lie down on a pair of beds, though she fretted that even the beds might be contaminated. Eli presented the adults a young goat he discovered wandering about, and they decided to take the risk of slaughtering it and cooking its flesh. Georgi slashed it cleanly across the neck, letting the blood pour into a pail.

"I can use that blood for a potion that will help the children recover," said Anna. "It might prevent the sickness in all of us."

She simmered the blood in a pot over an open fire, adding herbs and leeks from their food supply, and the roots of some beets Sara had found in a furrow. The mass slowly congealed into a lumpy concoction with an acrid, faintly sweet, smell.

"So, you think this will help to heal Aron and Sofi?" Georgi gazed at the pot dubiously.

"This is what my mother made when my brother and I were sick. We both grew to be strong and healthy. It's certainly worth trying."

Aron had become unconscious, his mind generating a spectacle of bright dreams and visions that guided him to the edge of life. His breath stopped; the glow of fever on his face faded to ashen grey.

Outside, they heard Wanda's wail. Daniel ran into the house.

"What is it? "Aron."

He lifted Aron's body and held it against his own, rocking back and forth. "Breathe!" he exhorted.

"Breathe!"

He held Aron's body firmly, pouring his strength into it, imploring him to live. Georgi and Anna came to the door and he gestured for them to stay outside.

"Breathe!"

Finally from Aron, a sharp inhalation. Daniel felt Aron's heart beating against his own, and his son's breath warm upon his neck. He set him down carefully and covered him.

Aron opened one eye weakly and beheld his father. "Papa," he murmured, and rolled onto his side and fell into a deep sleep.

The children lingered in the nether world between sickness and health for eight days, nursed by Wanda, who became pale and drawn, not with disease, but fatigue. On the eighth day, simultaneously, Sofi and Aron lost their skin blotches and their fevers cooled to normal temperatures.

Only they had contracted the typhus, which was owed, according to Anna, to the preventative power of her medicine. Mercifully, it had turned rancid after four days, and had to be thrown out.

Bounty they acquired from the farm included a store of

smoked jerky from the slaughtered goat, a basket of apples, a sack of fresh grain and a jug of vegetable bits for soup, that had been rendered from beets, onions and cabbage. Their water was replenished from a fresh stream, hay was tied onto the roofs of the wagons, and they were ready to move on.

Georgi had had a suspicion the plague was borne by lice, and he instigated a boil-down, scrub-down of clothing, blankets, their bodies, and the bodies of their horses. What lice they found were thrown into the fire.

Now in her fourth month of pregnancy, Sara's morning sickness had fallen away, and the bulge of her forming child was apparent. Increasingly, she felt a rapport, a deepening sense of maternity.

It was early November and still sunny though with a nip in the air. Each day gave way to darkness a little sooner.

They traveled well, perhaps twenty miles on the day after the interlude of sickness. The road surfaces were good and they passed an assortment of people who seemed healthy enough.

"Are we safe now?" asked Eli.

"I think so," said Georgi. "I think it's behind us."

Next afternoon, they stopped to fish at a rivulet where a group of women washing clothes were intrigued by the crosses on their wagons. The boldest asked who they were, and where they were going. When Georgi explained they were pilgrims headed to Rome to offer homage to the Pope and receive his blessing, she became very excited, gestured for them to wait, and ran off. She returned with a thin, pallid young priest with deep-set eyes and a limp that caused him to walk with a sideways lurch.

"I am honored to make the acquaintance of such devoted pilgrims as yourselves," he said. "Would you perhaps allow me to say a short mass by your caravan? This is as close to Rome and the Pope as the people of my parish will ever get."

Daniel pulled his beard ponderously and cleared his throat. "Well now, a mass, do you say? Hmmm, well, let me see."

"A moment please," said Georgi. "Please wait a moment."

He motioned for the families to follow him to a cluster of trees.

"The thing is," Georgi said, "we can't turn them down. It would look suspicious and it might be taken as an insult."

"But we are Jews," said Eli. "What will happen if we betray our faith?"

"We're not betraying anything," Georgi said. "Nothing bad will come of it. Have we been struck down because of these crosses? It would be a mitzvah, a good deed, to let these people have their ceremony."

"Do we agree? Good, then."

"Kneel when everyone else does, and cross yourselves when everyone else does. It won't be hard. If we look unusual to them, they'll just think it's because we're foreign blockheads."

He walked back to the priest.

"That's fine, father. We'd be happy and honored to have you hold a mass by our wagons,"

"Excellent," said the priest. "Please allow me a short time to summon the villagers and return. This is a great day."

Before the auspicious event began, they fished six trout

from the stream and cleaned them for the evening meal.

The priest returned wearing a surplice over his robe, and accompanied by a dozen boys in white smocks. Straggling alongside and behind were a hundred or so villagers of varying ages.

When they settled down, the priest explained this would be a low mass whose purpose it was to send their greetings and respect to God's earthly link in Rome. He placed candles and incense on an altar, an old woman lit them, and the priest began chanting in Latin. He paused, and the choir boys chanted a response. He read verses from the Bible, interspersed with more chanting and more responses The travelers, awkward at first, followed suit with reasonable grace. For Wanda, who had attended Sunday mass as a child, the ceremony evoked memories of people packed into a small church offering obeisance to a God who frightened her.

In unison, the priest and congregants intoned verses from the Sermon on the Mount:

Blessed are the meek, for they will inherit the earth.

Blessed are the merciful, for they will be shown mercy.

Blessed are the pure in heart, for they will know God.

Dramatically, the priest concluded a recitation of the Lord's Prayer, raising his arms, and gazing heavenward:

"DELIVER US FROM EVIL!"

After a pause, the choir sang a hymn and the congregants lined up to receive the bread and wine offering of the Host.

When it was over there were handshakes, embraces, well wishes. Daniel, more than the others, was surrounded with people eager to pat his back and bestow benedictions in phrases he could barely understand.

"Yes, yes," he responded. "Fine. Thank you. Good day to you."

As the travelers resumed their journey the next morning, the priest and his flock lined the road to wave and wish them godspeed. A young woman close to Sara's age handed her a wreath of wildflowers and pointed to Sara's abdomen and her own.

"Yes, I see," said Sara. "It's for the baby. And you're having a baby too."

"It's strange, this showering of love," said Eli. "If they had known we were Jews, what then? They might have ignored us or chased us with pitchforks."

"But they didn't, and we had a pretty good time here," said Georgi. "Better to be live imposters than dead martyrs."

"The sun shines on both."

"You're catching on," said Georgi.

In Bohemia, the men and boys hired on to work for a month digging ore at an iron mine. The work was hard, the days long, the pay very good.

Most of the regular mine workers had been drafted into a fighting force to deflect a Hungarian attack on the Empire in the southeast. Prince Anton, a grandson of King Wenceslaus IV, owned the mine and had had no choice but to lend his workers to the emperor's army, an imperative that grieved and enraged him. Profits had slowed abruptly to a trickle, profits that would be used to build a splendid new castle for his young wife, Princess Carla of Austria.

The prince was resigned to the fact he would never have more political power than he had, or own more land than he did, but he could achieve greatness by building the most spectacular castle in the kingdom, perhaps in all the world. Most Importantly. it would please the princess, who missed the luxury of her native Vienna, the social flux, the titillating gossip of court life, the subtle changes of fashion and manners. At twenty, she lamented she was sacrificing her youth to become a pretender among bumpkins, an elite foreigner forced to adapt to a new life that frightened her.

Anton, fifteen years older than her and staunch in his devotion, found her petulance as charming as it was dismaying, and was determined to make her happy, no matter the cost.

The royal court at Prague did not make her happy. Plots within King Podebrand's government and external threats from the Empire rendered Bohemia's court rocky and conspiratorial, far removed in sophistication from the glittery halls of Vienna. As high-born royalty, the prince and princess were sought-after guests at the receptions and amusements of Prague's aristocracy, but they attended them infrequently; Carla was uncomfortable in the midst of Prague's nobility and was having a struggle with their language. She suspected some of the women were mocking her, but wasn't deft enough in their nuances to be sure.

To relieve her homesickness, she and the prince had traveled twice to Vienna. After the second trip, they returned with a younger sister, a favorite cousin, a Pomeranian dog, a pair of love birds in a wicker cage. They had also brought back a cat that slipped away somewhere between the Danube and Eggenburg, altering its destiny in the pursuit of a mouse.

The prince had managed to replace half his miners with the lure of high pay. The bursar was instructed to distribute, each week, ten percent of the value of ore extracted. Each worker would receive according to his results; the more he dug, the more he got.

The foreman, a bald, mustachioed behemoth named Milic, approached Daniel's wagon as he and Aron were replacing a broken wheel, a short distance from the mine. He spoke slowly, in a gravelly voice, gesturing toward the vast open pit. Daniel shrugged, and asked him, "Do you speak Polish?" Milic grunted, raised his hands to indicate a pause, and went off. He returned with a small, sinewy man of about fifty. The man was shirtless, sweaty, dusty.

"Yes. They call me Viktor. My wife was raised in Krakow and so I know your language. It is not a happy marriage but I'll get to the point. Milic, here, is the boss of this mine. He says you can all work, the fathers and the sons, and you will be paid every week in coins. What do you want to do? Do you want to work?"

"How much pay is good pay?" asked Georgi? Viktor explained the prince's ten percent plan.

"If you work hard, it's plenty," he said. "Already I have bought a horse, a cow, new tools. My wife went to Prague and bought fine wool for our winter clothing."

"What do you think?" Daniel asked. "It wouldn't hurt to stop for a while and earn some good money."

"We'd need a house," said Wanda, "so we don't have to stay cramped in the wagons all the time."

Anna and Sara chirped in agreement.

"Well then, tell Milic we'll be glad to work, but only for a month," said Daniel, "because we want to get moving again before Europe freezes over. And we'll need a house to live in."

Viktor interpreted it to Milic, who nodded cheerfully, and responded.

"He says you can start tomorrow," said Viktor. "He said he knows a man, his own cousin, who will rent you a house at a very reasonable price."

Their abode was at the base of a small mountain hovering over a lake that loons and geese would soon abandon for warmer climates.

Draped in a shawl against the morning chill, Sara sat on a log watching wavelets lap the shore in a gentle rhythm as she communed silently with the child within.

"I had a baby once."

Wanda appeared beside her as though she had materialized from nowhere. "But he died."

"I'm sorry. What happened?"

"This is between only you and me."

"All right."

"When I was sixteen I fell in love with a Prussian cavalry officer. That was many years ago when Gdansk belonged to the Teutonic Knights. My father had brought us there from a farm near Posen because a terrible flood ruined our crops and drowned our animals. He found work as a shipfitter and we moved into a rickety house near the waterfront. When it rained there were puddles on the floor and the wind blew through cracks in the wall and we would all cough and sniffle. But my father and brothers fixed it up with strong wood and built a fireplace as big as the one we had on the farm.

"I was happy in that cozy home in the city, with my family; it was an exciting place for a girl who came from a farm. There were sailors and foreigners from everywhere, Danes, Swedes, Germans, English, French, Spaniards. Sometimes I saw dark-skinned people from Africa and Arabs from the Holy Land. Rich people rode around in fancy carriages. After a while we were pretty well off. My brothers got work loading ships and my mother baked pastries that I sold at a little stand near the docks. My mother warned me that when men flirted and made brash proposals I should be calm and ignore them. That was easy until Fritz began coming by in his scarlet uniform with his sword, his mustache, his shiny brown eyes. Each time he bought a pastry he would give me a little extra and he would touch my palm when he paid.

"It got so I thought about him all the time, and on days he didn't come, I feared that I would never see him again.

"One day he told me he was being sent to a cavalry troop in Konigsberg in a week's time and asked if I would walk with him that evening. We walked with my arm in his and we talked, and he bought me flowers. We went to his room in the officers' quarters and he spread a blanket by the fireplace and we, well, you know, we embraced. We did that every evening until he had to leave. He promised he would come back in a month to get me and bring me to Konigsberg and marry me.

"Waiting that month seemed like ten years and when the month passed he didn't come. Three more weeks went by and still he didn't come. I couldn't stand waiting anymore, so I took some money from my mother's metal box, told my brother Kazimir everything and hired a carriage driver to take me to Konigsberg.

"He wasn't there or anywhere else, he was dead. The colonel of his regiment told me Fritz' entire troop had been trapped and killed by Cossacks during a campaign in Russia.

"I got light-headed then and fainted. I woke up in a bed in someone's attic and I became frantic and started screaming. The colonel and a woman came in, gave me a cup of milk with vodka, talked to me until I was calm, and I fell back to sleep.

"The colonel's wife told me I could work for them as a maid and stay in the attic if I wanted. I only wanted to die but I stayed there and worked for them. When I wasn't working I would sit in my room and weep or stare at the wall. One day I began to swell with a baby and I stopped feeling so miserable. They gave me lighter duties and told me I could keep living there and have the baby there, and the baby would be like their grandchild.

"I named him Fritz after his father. He nursed well and was very beautiful and healthy.

The colonel and his lady were very sad when I told them I was returning to Gdansk to join my family, but the colonel gave me some extra money and sent us home in a wagon escorted by two soldiers.

"It had been almost a year since I had seen my family. When I got to the house at Gdansk a strange woman answered the door. She said my parents had bought another small farm near Posen, and moved into it the month before.

"So I went there with Fritz, expecting a warm welcome and was met instead with coldness as though I was a stranger and a disgrace. During my absence the feeling between my parents and me had come loose and been replaced with resentment. They were unforgiving and tolerated me only because they had affection for their grandchild. Two months went by and I couldn't stand it anymore, so Fritz and I rode to Gdansk with a farmer who was bringing vegetables to the marketplace.

"To make this short, we stopped to relieve ourselves and the farmer tried to force himself on me. I said no, and he kept grabbing at me until I lost my temper, slapped him, kicked him between the legs and walked away with Fritz and our bundle. The farmer was furious, screaming at me, but I kept walking. He came back in a little while, threw a fine wool blanket down, and said, 'Keep it, you can have it.' I thought maybe it was his way of apologizing. We had a long walk ahead and we would need to stop and sleep.

"He came back again, this time with a constable on horseback. He yelled, 'That's her!

She's the one who stole my blanket!'

"I was arrested, convicted and put in a workhouse for a year that would become the third home for Fritz and me. I worked in a big room with forty other women, sewing clothes all day. Some of them had babies too, and I made friends, so it wasn't too bad.

"There was one woman named Helga who was crazy. She was so crazy they took her baby away and gave it to a family in Thorn. She talked to herself all the time and yelled angry things into the air that nobody could understand. Her job was to sweep and mop. She couldn't do anything harder than that.

"The end of this, the part I want to forget but keep remembering over and over, is that Helga stole my baby one day, and disappeared. It was February, freezing cold outside, with snow up to the windows.

"The staff let me help search the stockade and the garden but we couldn't find them anywhere. We went outside the gate and saw wheel tracks and footprints leading into the woods. It looked like she had slipped out the gate behind the supply wagon. We followed the tracks until one of the guards said, 'I see them.' Helga was sitting under a tree cradling the baby under her arms. They were both blue, frozen to death."

Wanda stopped talking and she and Sara sat quietly, staring into the lake. Sara placed her hands lightly over her abdomen to comfort the creature forming in her.

"I'm so glad you're with us, Wanda."

"Thank you. It's the best time of my life."

"You will dig this ore and put it in this cart. When the cart is full other men will hitch it to the mules and pull it away. You will fill another cart. I will keep track of all the carts for your pay."

This was spoken by Milic and rendered into Polish by Viktor. The neophyte diggers leaned on their picks and waited.

"You will work now," said Milic.

They worked for five hours, alternately picking and shoveling. Eli and Aron thought it great fun to toil alongside Daniel like grown men, though their enthusiasm dwindled to a trickle before the third cart.

"Where is the prophet to lead us out of captivity?" asked Eli.

"Let the prophet wait a month, until we get our pay," Daniel answered.

They were given thick soup, bread and cheese for lunch, devoured it hungrily, and collapsed into deep and profound slumber.

Their neighboring workers, a middle-aged German and a young Bohemian, saw the opportunity for a prank. When they were sure the Poles were asleep, they tied their ankles together with a strand of rope and waited to see what would happen.

Viktor announced the end of lunch time. "Everybody back to work now."

The exhausted novices lay inert, slowly focusing their awareness on the terraced strip mine around them.

"Well, we have to do it," said Daniel.

"Wake up. Get up!"

Daniel rose to his feet, took a step, was tripped by the rope. He fell sideways, landing on his shoulder, narrowly missing Aron. Aron, Georgi and Eli were jerked forward several yards. Now, abruptly, violently, they were wide awake.

"What the devil?"

"Son of a pig!"

The high-pitched braying of their neighbors made it obvious they had been victims of a trick. They untied the knots with cranky deliberation as Daniel briefed them in a low voice: "When we get the rope off, we're going to run to their cart and push it over. We have to show these donkeys what's what."

They got up, ran, and overturned the half-filled cart of ore.

"What are you doing?" yelled the German. "You've destroyed our work!"

"You like jokes?" replied Georgi. "That was a joke. Now everybody is happy. Everybody has made a joke."

The German tackled Daniel and they rolled around grappling and grunting in the dust.

The Bohemian started to lunge but backed off when Georgi held up his hand as a warning to stay put.

Viktor called to them: "Milic is coming. Get on your feet. Get to work."

Milic stood before them bellowing a salvo of deprecations. The wrestlers parted. He beckoned for Viktor to come forward, roared some words, and walked off.

"He says he hates troublemakers. He says everyone will work now and if there is any more trouble, he will make even bigger trouble."

They worked four more hours until dark, filling two

more carts, slowed by fatigue, aching muscles, blisters.

"Milic says you will work!" said Eli.

"Milic!" said Aron. "I'll give you Milic. Milic schmilic!"

"Brilliant," said Eli. "The words of a poet!"

Not that their castle was shabby; it was quite fine, a handsome edifice of stone on a rise overlooking a panorama of forest, valley and river. Their bedchamber opened to a terrace of polished tiles, carved benches, statues, flowerboxes, a sundial. The previous emperor, Sigismund, had secluded himself in the castle during a riotous period and proclaimed, in a fanciful moment, that it was a jewel in the crown of the Holy Roman Empire.

In Anton's estimation, though, it was not very remarkable. He promised Carla he would build in its place a marvel worthy of her beauty, and described how it would be resplendent in marble, oriental wood, alabaster, stained glass, a moat prowled by lions, and moorish gardens graced with pools and fountains.

Meanwhile, he was preparing the way, accumulating profits from the mine and exchanging ideas with his architect, Mathias. They had been comrades at the University of Paris where along with the arts and sciences, they had studied Parisiennes, wine, and self-indulgence. Mathias had shed enough of the latter to emerge as a talented if obscure artist. The prince's messenger had located him in a rundown section of Prague after a frustrating week of inquiring and searching.

When Anton described his vision, Mathias was exhilarated.

"Do I accept? Do birds fly? You have given purpose to a squandered, meaningless life."

Immersion in Anton's project eased Mathias' craving for strong drink and allayed a recent plummet into self pity. Absorption in a thousand details occupied his waking hours, and nightly, his dreams teemed with parapets, arches, towers, gardens, a great hall. Mornings, he and Anton met in the planning room to analyze and modify his drawings, considering matters of size, shape, location, aesthetics. It looked as though six months might be required just to conceive the final design, render acceptable models, and receive the peripatetic delivery of building materials.

When the prince's servant found him, Mathias had been on the verge of suicide, contemplating whether to take poison, hang himself, or fling himself off a balcony. His woman Tanya had left him for a widowed coffin maker whose attraction it seemed, was his ordinariness, his bland sanity that made no demands on her except nightly copulation. Ten years of Mathias' emotional peaks and valleys had at first excited her, then occupied her, and finally, left her drained of vitality. She'd lost the will to cope any longer with his demands, his psychic storms, his overweening brilliance. The coffin maker, Gregor, meant peace, a comfortable income. She could find out who, if anybody, she was.

Mathias' plan to beat the man and reclaim Tanya as his own was a spectacular failure. Gregor knocked him out with one punch, carried him back to his studio, flung him onto his bed, and not so dull after all, splattered him with blue and red paint.

A troubling effect of her leaving was that Mathias became obsessed with her like a young man in love and craved her more than ever before. Thoughts of her filled him with a glow, an expansion that was almost unendurable. He attempted to exorcise it in work, painting pictures of her in bright, garish, colors and slashing them to pieces. He carried the tattered portraits to an alley and set fire to them in the company of a pair of vagrants who shared their wine with him, enjoying the warm blaze as he wept and moaned.

"You've got to understand you're better off without her," one of them observed. "You've got to realize women are no damn good."

"Nothing is any damned good in this filthy quagmire of a world, There's no good in anything at all. That's why I'm going to kill myself."

It was in this morbid condition that Prince Anton's man had found him.

Rabbi Moshe Mordecai, a rabbi and surviving adult male of a small village near Breslau, recommended to Daniel and Georgi that they paint over the crosses on the wagons and be who they were—advice that was declined.

"Why should we be bait for murderous fanatics?" asked Georgi. "You know what happens; you've been through it."

That was so. A rabid Jew hater, Giovanni of Rome, legate of Pope Nicholas V, had stirred up mobs with powerful sermons that accused Jews of killing Christian children and desecrating the Host. He employed torture and threats to wrest false confessions and justify his lust for killing. Forty Jews were burned at the stake at Breslau. Moshe's village was besieged by a frenzied mob that hanged the adult males and forcibly baptized their children.

After Moshe had dangled a few moments, the leader of the executioners sliced through his rope with a sword. He lay on the ground gasping for air as his rescuer kicked his ribs and spit on him.

"Tell the world, filthy Jew," he said.

He lifted Moshe to his feet, held a knife to his throat and forced him to watch his son die. Moshe fainted and fell at his son's feet.

That had been eight years before. Moshe decided there was no God and he ceased to be a rabbi. He wandered to Prague where Zinna, an older sister who had married a blacksmith and converted to Christianity, took him in.

For a year, Moshe rarely ventured outside the house. He spent much of his time writing a convoluted dissertation that disproved the existence of God and refuted all the tenets of Judaism. Paradoxically, he spoke continually to the God he no longer believed in, often screaming in rage, and he issued a challenge: "If you exist, if you are offended, then strike me dead."

Zinna's husband Kurt thought Moshe was completely mad and feared he would bring God's wrath on all of them if he continued with his raging diatribe. He wanted to turn him out but Zinna refused adamantly, reasoning that Moshe had nowhere to go, and needed care.

On a snowy night on the bridge over the Vltava river, God answered, as Moshe watched snowflakes fall and dissolve into the river. His thoughts spiraled into utter silence and an understanding of timeless being came to him clearly and brightly.

An awareness settled in that his purpose in this world was to serve the Spirit by serving his fellow humans.

He established relations with the Jewish community, began assisting and teaching at the Prague synagogue and made it his practice to seek and counsel Jews who lived among the Lower Tatra mountains, where he encountered the band from Kletki.

He came upon Eli drawing water from a well, noticed the Semitic cast of the boy's features, and surmised that he came from a shtetl community somewhere.

"Shalom," he said. "Can you spare some water for the parched throat of a rabbi?" Eli offered the bucket and ladle.

"What is a rabbi doing in these mountains where there is no shul or synagogue?"

"Truly speaking," said Moshe, "a synagogue is any place where you are open to God, and a shul is whatever points you in that direction. But to ordinary minds, they are just certain places with ordinary meanings. Look at the power of that mountain, the majesty of this lake and that meadow. Do you think men could build a better tabernacle with hammers and saws? Everywhere, it's a house of worship. God breathes into every speck of the universe."

"But not always into men's hearts, rabbi," said Georgi.

Approaching quietly, he overheard the conversation.

"Why do men have such black hearts, rabbi?" asked Eli.

"We fear and we hate and we are poisoned by it," said Moshe. "Our special task in this world is to let the Spirit flow through us and dissolve our wickedness."

Moshe noticed the approach of a man leading a horse, and his face lit up with a smile of recognition.

"Look! Here comes one who knows the tabernacle of nature. Peace, cousin!" called Moshe, "Peace upon you!"

Daniel passed the reins to Aron and walked toward the rabbi, squinting curiously.

His eyes crinkled in joyous recognition. "It's you!" he said. "It's Moshe!"

They embraced and laughed uproariously, doing an impromptu stomp dance, like a pair of demented bears.

"It's been how long? Twenty years?"

"At least," said Moshe. "We moved to Breslau when I was only fifteen years old."

"It's amazing, amazing!" said Daniel. "This is Moshe, the son of my mother's brother.

We used to wrestle like bear cubs, swim in the river, hike to the mountain caves. It was his special job to tap my head when I fell asleep during lessons in shul."

"I always thought if Daniel could have stayed awake for five minutes at a time, he might have become the greatest Torah scholar the world has ever known."

"I preferred sleep," said Daniel. "But that honor might go to our friend here. He can recite torah backwards. He can sing it in German and rhyme it in Russian."

"A fancy story," said Georgi. "The truth is I plod through the Hebrew like a well intentioned half-wit."

Moshe emitted a booming laugh.

"Who isn't a half-wit when trying to grasp the elusive mysteries of torah?"

At dinner that night Moshe went over the years since he'd last seen Daniel, his studies at the synagogue in Breslau, his work as a rabbi. He related how his wife had been struck and killed instantly by lightning.

"A violent death, but quick, and in its way, merciful. She had been suffering from a disease of the joints so painful she could hardly walk."

He recounted how the Inquisition had come to Breslau soon after that, and the savagery that came with it. Trying to describe the hanging, his voice broke and his face became soaked with tears.

"And so Chaim, he struggled and choked, and I couldn't break loose to help him." Wanda moved behind him and placed her hands on his shoulders.

They sat quietly, watching the flickering candles create a sad play of light and shadow, Daniel, Wanda, Aron, Sara, Georgi, Anna, Eli, Sofi and Moshe.

"Well," said Daniel, "stay with us. You can come to Spain with us, if you like."

The third week of mining, the stimulation of a cold December wind and occasional flurries of snow spurred them to work harder and faster. The ore piled up faster in the carts and the mules pulled it away sooner.

At the end of each day they were simply tired, in contrast to the aching exhaustion they had suffered in the beginning.

The blisters had become calluses and their muscles bulged firmly. Eli and Aron were eating nearly double their usual amount, and the hard labor had added a sinewy, mature look to them that belied their fourteen years. Daniel's pot belly had withered to a forgotten leanness that required new holes on his belt strap.

They worked even on the traditional sabbath, it being supposed they were Christians.

They were earning enough pay that by converting it into jewels and adding it to their cache, they should be able to start their new lives in Spain without concern for money.

Evenings before supper, Georgi and Moshe would read and discuss segments of the Talmud with Eli and Aron. Aron had a practical, skeptical frame of mind like Daniel, and like him, was content to see the world as it appeared, free of interpretations and ostensible meanings. When Moshe chided Aron's seeming indifference one evening, Daniel interjected, "What do you expect? The son of a camel driver is a camel driver. If you can make such a person into a scholar, fine, you're welcome to try."

"Maybe we can make a camel driver into one who contemplates the mystery of each grain of sand," said Moshe.

"Maybe he can do that," said Aron, "without needing scripture."

A theological dispute was born, long or short on hortatory according to the bent of the arguer, and was terminated, happily, by the aroma of dumplings and stew.

Wanda asked the wise ones to clear the table so they could eat.

Princess Carla considered projects that might alleviate her boredom: She could take a lover but Anton was as much of a lover as she needed, or wanted. She could host a gathering from Prague but the idea chilled her and gave her flutters. She thought it might be amusing to select furniture for the new castle, but it wouldn't be completed for two more years. What, then, would have flair to it?

She regarded her reflection in the birdbath and saw a blonde, blue-eyed princess of the House of Hapsburg, a beauty by most standards. She struck the water and watched the image break up into concentric circles, ripple, and form back into her face.

Her sister and cousin had returned to Vienna the previous day, taking traveler's advantage of a sunny break in the weather. That left her with Anton, the servants, and her dog Sak. There was also Mathias, who emerged sporadically from his workroom looking disheveled, abstracted, and in her estimation, quite mad.

"I see a princess, a dog and a birdbath. A pretty picture."

Mathias was behind her, his face shimmering in the water and merging with hers. She moved so that his whole face was visible. He was a strange looking man, she thought, with his long crooked nose, pitted, sallow skin, and unruly black hair that stuck out in every direction.

"So. It's you. Our artist has left his place of creation. What have you accomplished today?"

"I'm working on some arches for the hallway that spans the bedchambers. I think they will make that part of the castle friendlier, more welcoming. Come take a look. Maybe you will have suggestions or bitter complaints. With Anton at the mine today, you can be my goad."

The large oak table was strewn with charcoal drawings, painted pictures, and geometrical patterns marked with mathematical equations. The colorful drippings of paint jars stacked on a shelf gave the room a semblance of jollity. Carla's attention was drawn to an imaginative rendering of the castle as it would look when completed. It had the allure of the magical kingdoms of storytellers. Each stone and turret gleamed in a kind of translucent glory in rich, clear colors. Perched on the hilltop, it seemed almost ready to rise and float into an infinite, sparkling sky.

"Well, tell me what you think." said Mathias

"I'm pleased with this, very pleased. If you and Anton can really do this, it'll be a wonder. It's like heaven."

"Of course you have to realize there'll be a difference between this and the actual castle, but this is what we're aiming for. This is what I want you to feel."

"But what am I to do until then?"

She blushed, embarrassed by the sudden revelation of ennui to a man she didn't really know.

"Do? What do you mean? What do you usually do?"

"I talk to the servants and I stroll and I ride my pony. I make a silly quilt and I look out the windows and feel homesick for Vienna."

"Well, I don't know. I don't know what to tell you. Everybody finds life tedious sometimes. Myself, there have been times I've stared at the wall for days on end and not had enough oomph to cook my dinner or take a walk. This is what happens. Don't let it get you down."

It was a relief. Since she'd been married, she'd not put words to the quandary of feeling vapid, of feeling frozen in the role of an aristocratic wife in an aristocratic castle. It was like walking on a pleasant road that went endlessly in a circle.

"Look. I have a plan," said Mathias. "Let's pretend I'm your wizard and I say, 'You know how to sew? Wonderful. Take this picture and make a tapestry of it for the great hall.'"

"You don't need it?"

"Not for now. Let's say I'm your oracle as well as your wizard and I look into the future and see that you will soon have children and be busy and fulfilled and have many friends."

"Well, all right. Let's say that. There's no harm in saying it."

On the terrace, she propped the picture on a chair and studied it. She would need a lot of thread in many colors. She would ask Anton to take her to Prague to buy thread.

Several days before their period of mining was to be completed, a heavy snowstorm set in, so severe they couldn't leave the house. A howling wind battered and taunted the log walls outside the house and blew drifting snow into rapid, dancing flurries. Heavy clumps of it slid off overburdened branches and crashed dramatically onto the roof.

Spiked icicles dangled ominously from the eaves like frozen swords. Winter had stormed in, laid siege, and conquered.

They burned logs, ate, slept, played cards and chess, studied scripture, mended clothes, chatted. Each morning, a man and boy bundled up to go to the stable and tend the horses, bringing with them a pot of boiled water to thaw the drinking trough that had frozen into a block of ice. They brushed and rubbed the animals, cinched up their blankets and fed them their fodder. When they returned from the horse chores, they had patches of white on their eyebrows, whiskers and shoulders. Their cheeks and ears glowed red and they performed a hop dance to restore circulation to their limbs.

When the storm ended the sky was pale gray, the mountain was white, the valley below was blanketed in snow, and the little lake was covered with a sheet of ice.

"It looks like winter's come to stay," said Georgi, "and our mining days are over."

"And also your journey," said Moshe. "You can't cross Europe this time of year. You'll get caught in a blizzard and you'll freeze to death."

No one argued. They could envision the bleakness of being trapped by wheel-high snow in the middle of nowhere with dwindling provisions, pregnant Sara to protect, and the possibility of thieving, murderous thugs lurking about.

"The way I see it," said Daniel, "we could settle in here, or we could go on to Prague with Moshe and find a place to stay. What do you think? Which do you like better?"

The appeal of a large sophisticated city prevailed over the prospect of a cozy but monotonous seclusion on a mountain. The women thought it especially agreeable that they could stroll, sample the shops, perhaps even buy something. And Daniel pointed out the men could set up a workshop and make vessels to sell in Prague and other places along the way.

"But let's paint over the crosses on the wagons," said Georgi. "Moshe's right. Let's be who we are."

Aron and Eli were delegated to do the painting while Daniel and Georgi went to Milic's house to pick up their final pay and let his cousin know they would need the house for just a few more days.

Milic was uncharacteristically cheerful, greeting them with backslaps and hearty laughter, as though they were long-time comrades.

"Vodka!" he exclaimed, proffering a bottle. "Health!"

They repeated 'health" all around, swigged, and passed the bottle in a circle three times until it was empty. Two of Milic's smaller children caught up in the congeniality, shrieked and climbed onto his shoulders. He swung them in a wide arc to the floor as they yelled in mock hysteria and scrambled back on again.

Georgi, abuzz with the unaccustomed liquor, was speaking to Milic's cousin Dmitri, gesticulating, trying to explain they would soon be gone. Dmitri smiled uncomprehendingly, and shrugged his shoulders.

"I'm wondering how to say, 'leaving house' in Czech," said Georgi. "I wouldn't know," said Daniel. "Why don't you draw a picture?"

"Good idea. You're even shrewder when you're intoxicated."

He sketched a house on the hearthstones with a piece of charcoal. Alongside, he drew four suns, pointed at them and the house, and held up four fingers.

"Four days. We go. Four days."

Dmitri beamed in comprehension. He held up four fingers and emulated Georgi's words.

"Four days!"

This inspired a new bottle and a round of toasts to international understanding and cooperation. As the bottle circled, each quaffer exclaimed, "Four days!"

Outside, the cold air helped clear their minds, though they walked in a rambling zigzag, occasionally stumbling on unsuspected obstacles. Daniel dived for a hare that was leaping about spiritedly, missed, and landed face down in a snowbank. The creature paused to regard him curiously, and bounded off on urgent hare business.

"There goes fresh meat and a pair of gloves," said Daniel. "And my reputation as a hunter."

They heard laughter and turned to see Mathias and Viktor enjoying their folly.

Mathias affected a slight bow.

"Good day, my friends, I am Mathias of Prague, well known wastrel, friend of tormented hares, and architect to

Prince Anton, who reigns over this region. And you might be?"

Viktor rendered it into Polish.

"Tell him," said Georgi, "that we are Georgi and Daniel of Spain, holy vagabonds, philosophers, and emissaries to the court of His Eminence, the Puka of Spain."

Mathias told Viktor to ask if such illustrious emissaries could spare time this day to perform some work at the castle, which would reward them amply with pay and a profound sense of accomplishment.

Viktor explained that a small avalanche had caused a cascade of mud and scree, covering the bridge that spanned the creek in front of the castle, and Mathias was looking for men to help dig it out. Without the bridge, the castle was cut off, and no carriages could enter or leave. Most of the servants were too old or infirm to be of much help, or were women. The prince himself was working alongside the groundskeepers at that very moment, shoveling away energetically.

"Viktor, you found the right men," said Daniel. "We know enough about digging to dig out that bridge blindfolded with our legs tied and one hand waving at the sky. Show us the way!"

They trudged up the hill for half an hour until the wall of the castle came into view, and walked down a brief slope where, indeed, Prince Anton and two of his men were hurling shovelfuls of dirt away from the bridge. The prince, who affected sideburns and an elegant mustache, had an easy air of authority that set him apart from the servants. He was well over six feet tall, lean, with broad shoulders. He waved at the quartet walking toward him.

"Mathias! This is hard work! How lucky I was to be born a prince and not a peasant," he laughed. "Bring on your men."

The seven diggers had the bridge cleared in six hours, just before nightfall. By torchlight, they shored up a section that had been damaged and re-nailed some planks that had come loose. Princess Carla stood by with her pooch Sak, enjoying the uniqueness of the event, and the relaxed competence of her husband. As the men were finishing, she left to supervise the cooks in the preparation of a lavish meal.

They dined royally at the prince's table on goose, veal, bread, wine, cabbage, and pudding.

"Look here," said Anton, "it's dark outside, getting colder, and there are wolves about. You'd better stay here tonight. There's plenty of room."

As they settled in to sleep, Georgi said, "You know, they're probably wondering what happened to us."

"True," said Daniel, "but we'll have a good story to tell."

In Prague, Moshe's sister Zinna found them a house on her street that had been vacated when its owner, a very old man, dropped dead on his way to mass. It could adequately house no more than six, so Moshe brought Sara and Aron into his sister's house with him. Her husband Kurt gave up sulking when he recognized he enjoyed having the youngsters around; they were relatives, after all, and pleasant enough. He made space in his blacksmith shop for Daniel and Aron to work at their carving trade, and the shelf above their bench slowly acquired piles of platters, bowls and goblets that Georgi and Eli carried to market to peddle, when the weather allowed.

Wanda and Anna had a loud imbroglio one night over what to cook and how much, that sent Georgi and Daniel scampering to the comparative peace of a tavern, where they got into a shoving match with a couple of drunks who declared that all Poles were idiots.

Daniel, made philosophical by fumes of spirits, opined that "Two beautiful women under the same roof will have to hiss at each other and let sparks fly."

"But not often, let us pray," said Georgi.

The women made up after a couple of days of icy hauteur, and harmony was restored. They worked out a routine of alternating sovereignty wherein each would take turns cooking and have authority beyond appeal.

Zinna and Kurt were told the circumstances of Sara's pregnancy and agreed not to speak of it. The official explanation for neighbors and other outsiders was that her husband had died while serving as a soldier.

She liked that story. She could spin endless visions of it to suit her moods and fancies. In each version he died a hero, lying in a patch of roses, gazing at a warm blue sky. Before he murmured his last, he uttered her name. Sometimes the story frightened her, times when she would see his death so vividly that it seemed real, as though she herself were lying in his place. The sun would swell up hugely, radiating golden waves, and hurtle down and extinguish him/her in an ocean of light.

The imaginary soldier—she called him Gabriel—came to seem more real than Count Ozo Stefanek. The memory of coupling in the count's overpowering embrace would never leave her. It came to mind often but had been transformed into something impersonal, a cataclysmic force of nature that descended as an agent for some design of fate beyond her grasp. There were fires, floods, plagues, earthquakes, famines, and there was the count. She had heard Moshe say that God masks himself sometimes in terrible disguises, and that terrible moments have in them the seed of holiness.

If the count was the mindless force, Gabriel was the lover, the swain of her heart. He was clear and warm, attentive, comprehending. They took long walks in the countryside and shared their thoughts, no matter how intimate. On moonlit nights they embraced on the pungent earth as stalks of wheat swayed gently in the wind.

In her vision, she would see him riding off to war on a dark stallion, light reflecting blindingly off his armor. Strangely, his face would alternate between that of Gabriel and that of Count Ozo Stefanek.

"Psst. In here. Wise Maria will read your fortune. She knows the past. She knows the future. Wise Maria knows all."

The young woman who beckoned wore a magenta dress, golden earrings, a black scarf on her neck. Her eyes were dark as the hair that flowed onto her shoulders in ringlets.

"Come into the tent. Wise Maria will read your palms and explain your lives. She will help you."

The tent was pitched between a pair of colorfully painted caravans on the eastern edge of the city on a field fronting the river. A swarthy man sat on a tree stump, whittling on a piece of wood as he watched the Polish women indolently. A gray-haired woman and two young girls were singing a song in some exotic language and clapping their hands. Nearby, a man whose age was somewhere between eighty and a hundred, was showing a boy the proper way to mount a horse.

"These people are Gypsies," said Wanda. "I've seen their kind before, in Posen and Gdansk."

At that, the tent flap opened and Wise Maria stood before them.

"So you're from Poland. We too have lived in Poland. Come inside." The three women hesitated a few moments, and went in.

Within, there were carpets over the hard mud floor and a low table surrounded by cushions. On the table was a bowl of pink-colored water, a smooth egg-shaped rock, and two candles burning brightly. Wise Maria was dressed in a similar manner to the young woman who had greeted them except she wore no shoes. She was perhaps forty years old, quite beautiful, her tannish complexion set off with slightly greying black hair.

She sat cross-legged at the table and motioned for the others to sit, too.

"We liked Poland more than it liked us. Always, we were driven out of places because we were different. When a soldier reached into my blouse one day, I spit in his face and called my man Vlad. Vlad killed that pig with a knife and we left Poland forever. Soon, we go to Italy, where people like us are not bothered so much. But now we will talk about you. Like us, you are on a journey. To a southern country. Is that true?"

Anna replied that it was. "How did you know? We've never seen you before."

"I have knowledge that is hidden from others. My grandmother, who was a great seer, helped me open the third eye so that I can see into the past and future. I can reveal that which is hidden, but first you must give me three pfennig, one from each of you. The telling of a fortune has no power unless it is paid for."

They conferred silently, with narrowed eyes, and nodded in agreement. Each removed a pouch from her skirt waist and took out a coin.

"Good. Now we can proceed. I can envision your fourney and warn you of difficulties that may arise. But you must do this now: Put a finger in this sacred water, and onto your forehead. Put your lips to this stone. And then, pass your hands quickly over the candle flames."

They did as Maria bade them.

"For a short while now, we will relax our bodies and be quiet."

They felt a peaceful, soothing quality in Maria's gaze as she studied first Anna, then Wanda. She observed Sara longer than the others, with keen interest.

"In a month, you will continue your journey, on the same day as us. I recommend you travel with us as far as

Italy. We know the ways of the road. I see there are hazards if you travel alone: robbers and drunken soldiers, cruel and violent peasants. But please do not use the impolite word 'Gypsies.' We are Romany. You are Jewish?"

They nodded.

"Then time is favoring you, because after you leave this city there will be an attack on the Jews of Prague, and the house of worship will be vandalized."

"You two"—she nodded toward Anna and Wanda—"must avoid any more quarreling, at least until you reach Spain. I see that a serious quarrel can divide your families and put you in danger."

"And you,"—addressing Sara— "you have one in your womb who will be exceptional among men. In serving to turn people away from hatred and ignorance, he will be one of the inner teachers who appear in this world rarely and are poorly understood. There are some who will resent his teachings and seek to destroy him but you mustn't be afraid, the Power will watch over him."

As if to punctuate the prophecy, the being in Sara's womb stirred energetically. She answered with an affectionate pat.

As they walked back to their neighborhood, a light snow began falling. Church bells summoned worshipers to Sunday mass. Maria watched the three women recede into the distance until they were spectral.

Vlad, afflicted with the bane of jealousy, was relieved to see that the Polish men had women of their own; he wouldn't have to suffer the suspicious anger that clouded his judgment and made him feel sick. He knew his intense feeling for Maria ws not good for him but he was powerless to change it. Twice, he had killed men for daring to touch her, and had bloodied another for talking to her in a suggestive way. That man had been the chief's son at an encampment in Hungary. The chief outlawed Vlad and ordered him to take his caravans and family elsewhere.

After twenty years of marriage and four children, Vlad was no less attracted to Maria than he had been in the beginning. She was sheer magic to him. That was both a blessing and a curse, he knew, but there it was.

Maria had no quarrel with it. How many women had husbands who remained ardent lovers? And were also strong and clever. Even in the leanest times, in the meanest places, Vlad could invent schemes to keep food in their stomachs and clothes on their backs. His projects included buying and selling horses, as well as making magic amulets, love potions, wicked-looking stilettos, and he was adept at casting spells and creating rainfall during droughts. Or so he claimed. For a reasonable price, he would share his alchemical powder with certain enterprising souls who were advised that if they sprinkled it on a mound of soil during a full moon and maintained a proper attitude, it would be transformed into a pile of gold. There was inevitable gain to be had in mining delusions and who could prove it wrong? People got something for their money even if it was no more than shiny flimflam.

While she was still a young bride, he established Maria's reputation as a seer by howling down the chimney of an elderly farmer in Poland. She had read in the farmer's palm that the ghost of his dead wife would soon pay him a visit. He laughed cynically and said that if it really happened, he would give her a nanny goat. That night the farmer was awakened by the howling sound of his name, "Slawek! Slawek!" He bolted up in bed, his heart pounding, and saw a light outside the window form the features of his dead wife and recede back into darkness. Next morning, he brought the goat to Maria and begged her to intercede so that the ghost would never appear again. Vlad pointed out that such a difficult negotiation with the spirit world would require the sum of not only one but two goats, and the farmer complied gratefully.

As time went by, such tricks became unnecessary. It developed that Maria did indeed have a knack for divining the future. An astonishing number of her predictions turned out to be accurate, and word spread of her uncanny power. She herself didn't know how she did it, except that at certain times, a certain feeling came over her, and the stream of a person's life became apparent.

On a sunny and windy day of February, they headed their wagons away from Prague and toward Genoa—eight Romany, seven Jews, and Wanda, not so definable. The first mile south, they encountered four mounted cavalry soldiers clopping along slowly, each with a woman behind him, her arms encircling his waist.

Their sergeant trotted his horse to Vlad's caravan and inquired who they were and where they were going. He and his woman appeared tipsy, apparently the result of sipping from a wine jug looped to the saddle.

"Who are you to ask?" retorted Vlad. Maria hissed at Vlad and shook her head.

"I am one of Podebrad's palace guards and I ask what I want to ask, and therefore, I ask who you are and where you are going."

The woman behind him giggled.

"We're travelers and we're traveling. We're traveling to Italy where the sun always shines and wine flows freely from fountains in the plazas and where soldiers don't bother honest people who are going about their business."

Hearing this, the sergeant looked like a vexed bull, uncertain whether to paw the ground or attack.

Maria saw it was time to intercede. "Look here, we have gifts for you."

She took eight amulets from a box behind the wagon seat, polished stone triangles affixed to leather thongs.

"Wear these around your necks and they will protect you from the devil. The devil's power is useless against these."

The sergeant accepted and passed them around so that there were four soldiers and four mistresses with magical devil deflectors draped from their necks.

"Well then, kind lady, you and your people can go on your way."

The men snapped their reins and the four wagons began

moving. The drunken soldiers and their tandem ladies provided a farcical sort of military escort for a while, veering off finally toward an abandoned barn for licentious frolic. The devil may have wanted to go in with them but he was just plain out of luck.

Mid-March, they halted at the edge of a town near Vienna where the street was congested by a boisterous crowd. A festive air among the celebrants was tinged with danger. Some were drinking and roughhousing, others shouted foul deprecations while packs of excited dogs ran among them snarling, getting into fights. The crowd's noisy attention was focused on a procession moving toward a plaza.

"Let's see what's happening," said Daniel.

They stopped the wagons at a field of weeds well removed from the mob.

"Go on and take a look," said Vlad. "I'll stay with the horses. The first man to get enough of a look can take my place."

As they walked off, he beckoned to his son. "You know what to do, Tony."

"Yes, papa."

The commotion was centered around a small bearded man garbed in a gown of rough cloth. On his head was a conical hat illustrated with demons and crescent moons. His chest and arms were cinched with a rope pulled by a huge constable who jerked the rope in such a way that the prisoner had to move in a jiggly trot to keep from tripping and falling. A squad of soldiers followed in parade formation with pikes at their shoulders.

Leading the procession was a contingent of priests and public officials, their expressions upright and stern. A drummer boy trailed the spectacle, beating a slow, gloomy cadence.

Georgi made his way through the crowd cautiously, balancing Sofi on his shoulders. "Where are they taking that man, papa?"

"I don't know Sofi, we'll see."

Georgi asked an onlooker to explain what was going on. That man, a respectable citizen sort, cocked his head suspiciously. He was well-dressed, had a beefy, florid complexion, and eyes that bulged as though he were apoplectic. He balanced himself with a silver-tipped cane and prefaced his words by spitting on the ground.

"Bender, that swine you see there, the one they're pulling on the rope, is an enemy of the Church and society. He has openly admitted to being a freethinker."

Georgi relayed this to Anna, who passed it on to the others. "A what?" asked Daniel.

"He said a freethinker," said Eli.

"Ask him what a freethinker is," said Wanda.

"What kind of foreigners are you that you've not heard of freethinkers?" His eyes seemed to bulge more, after Georgi's second inquiry.

"Is that Polish you were speaking? Is that what you are, Poles?"

"So we are," said Georgi. "We're traveling south toward the Mediterranean sea." The burgher spat on the ground again.

"We don't much like foreigners here. But I'll tell you, I'll tell you what a freethinker is. It's somebody who thinks he can decide for himself what the truth is. It's somebody who puts his own mind above the church, the state and the Holy Bible. That man was telling his students to disregard authority and think for themselves. He was poisoning their minds. And for that he's going to be pilloried so that all may scorn him."

The march ended at a low wooden platform. Bender was dragged to the pillory where his hands and legs were set into semi-circular openings. After a plank was lowered and locked into place, the crowd let out a roar of approval and the dogs increased their aggravated barking.

When the dignitaries had assembled on the platform, the mayor of the town read from a parchment scroll in a mellifluous singsong.

"Can you make it out?" asked Daniel.

"It's a proclamation," said Georgi. "It says that man Bender will have to stay there for five days. It says that if he ever again preaches freethinking, his tongue will be cut out."

When the mayor finished, the officials filed off the platform, leaving a soldier to stand guard. Several eggs and pieces of garbage were flung, landing on the platform, the prisoner's head, and the uniform of the soldier, who glowered, and raised his sword. The freethinker's conical hat had been knocked off by a cabbage and he gazed at it forlornly, averting his eyes from the crowd.

"I think we've seen enough," said Daniel. "Enough to want to leave this place," said Georgi.

"I don't need to see it," said Vlad, when they returned and described it. He put a hand on Tony's shoulder and guided him away from the others. "Let's see what you got."

Tony pulled from his coat four necklaces, two pendants, a pouch of coins and a red velvet cap.

"Good boy," said Vlad. "Here, keep this cap, it looks good on you. But don't wear it until we leave this place."

"Papa, that man they punished, can we get him out of there? Do you think we can go back when it's dark, and free him?"

Vlad glanced at his son with droll appreciation.

"It's possible. I'm not saying we can do it but it's possible. We'll see what it looks like."

He laughed and gave Tony a playful poke on the shoulder.

After supper, Vlad conferred with Georgi and Daniel about Tony's idea and they decided it was worth a try but stipulated it must be abandoned at any moment if it got too dangerous.

"Just the three of us. Everyone else will stay here," said Daniel. "And your uncle and the boys will have the horses hitched up, with the wagons ready to go."

"It was Tony's idea," said Vlad. "Tony will come with us."

An hour before dawn they walked quietly to the plaza. Except for a few drunks sleeping at doorways, the streets were deserted. As they approached the platform they saw Bender's body framed by the pillory and they saw that the soldier was on the ground beside him, sleeping..

Bender was awake, watching them warily. Daniel signaled him with a finger to his lips, to be quiet.

"All right, do it," Vlad whispered to Tony.

Tony slipped behind the soldier and removed his helmet. The soldier grunted, "Hey, what?" before Vlad hit him on the head with a club and he went limp.

"Don't worry, we're going to get you out of here," Georgi said to Bender, "In just a moment."

"I can't find the key," Vlad whispered in alarm. "No, wait, here it is, it's in his boot."

He passed it to Daniel who opened the lock, separated the pillory, and freed Bender. His face was besmirched with gobs of spit and there were bruises and dried blood where stones had hit him. His tangled gray hair was gooed with an egg that had been tossed at him.

"Help me up," he whispered. "My limbs are numb."

Vlad and Daniel steadied him and walked him a few steps, until his knees buckled.

Daniel kneeled and Georgi and Vlad set Bender onto Daniel's back so that he could carry him piggy-back.

"Hold on old man," Daniel said. "It's not far."

"I just thought of something," said Georgi. "Go on, I'll catch up with you."

He went stealthily back to the platform. The soldier was still out, lying in a heap.

Georgi lifted him, placed his hands and legs into the pillory and fastened the lock. "That'll teach you to be a freethinker and a troublemaker," he said.

When the morning sun broke through the clouds and brightened the plaza, the soldier gradually woke and looked about in bewilderment. It was a while before his buzzing, confused mind could sort things out and comprehend that he was locked in a pillory. He began yelling furiously and a couple of sleeping beggars were roused to walk over and see what was happening.

They buried Bender in a field east of the port of Genoa. The cold windy passage over alpine terrain had chilled him to the marrow and sickened him.

With nowhere else to go, he had traveled with his liberators, thinking that perhaps he could start afresh as a teacher of German, once he mastered the language of Spain.

Gasping for air as he lay by the fire, a congestion of fluid stressed his lungs until his heart could perform no more. The Romany women had been singing a song that asked God for his safe passage to the next world. Before he breathed a last breath and left for that world, he saw himself reflected in the amber of Maria's eyes.

They left his grave unmarked and strewn with wildflowers and they moved on to the coast.

It was mid-May, and the climate was warmer and gentler than any they had known since Poland. People they met had the usual curiosity about them but little of the truculence. They bought food from vendors and were content to camp near an inlet near the sea for a spell, washing their clothing, repairing the caravans, relaxing.

Sara, in her final month of pregnancy, had entered into a stage of euphoria, an utter satisfaction with forming a baby amid the invigorating sights and scents of the Mediterranean, and the caring family and friends she was with. She lay on her back watching clouds drift in a cobalt sky, and knew she would never regret leaving Kletki for this. It was as Eli had written in one of his poems:

Ask the lizard basking on the rock And he'll tell you Ahhh.

They went their separate ways at Genoa, the Romany heading for the region of Tuscany and the Poles booking passage on a ship bound for Barcelona.

Their parting meal was at a restaurant by the sea that Vlad insisted on hosting, with a gold necklace as payment. The proprietor was glad to accept and no one asked Vlad how he had got it.

Flagons of wine appeared and disappeared during the celebration and toasts were offered in a spirit of lighthearted pandemonium.

"What can I say?" asked Daniel "It's been a fine and difficult adventure. Here's to health and good fortune to every Romany in Europe for ten generations."

Georgi declared that the recording angel would inscribe this moment as a pinnacle in the saga of humanity.

Vlad rose unsteadily to offer his third and final toast. "My good friends, I...I..."

He wavered bravely, and collapsed onto the table, overturning a vase of flowers and sending chicken bones flying.

The celebrants contemplated Vlad's outstretched body

and cheered wildly. Wanda raised her glass for the final toast:
"Luck!"

"Luck!" they responded.

Aron stood at the prow, watching it part the waves into frothy spray. He had never known such happiness as at that moment on that ocean, the sunlight shimmering on the water, gulls swooping for quarry, the briny wind on his face, the sway of the ship. He resolved he would go to sea someday and become master of a vessel like this, whose sails touched the sky.

Below, Eli, ashen-faced, was vomiting into a bucket and moaning. Also seasick were Anna, Georgi, Daniel and Wanda, who managed to stagger topside and vomit off the side of the ship. The captain had assured them the sickness would run its course in a day or so and return no more.

"This happens every time. Look, some of my crew have it too."

Sure enough, several sailors were drooping over the rail and puking off the side.

The cabin next to the captain's had been reserved by a wealthy and important couple who changed their plans, and the captain provided it to Sara in deference to her ripe pregnancy.

"The young mama must be comfortable," he said.

It was furnished with two bunks, a writing table, a stool, a stand with a wash basin, a teakwood trunk. A porthole gave its occupants a view of the horizon, adorned with droplets of spray.

Sara asked the captain if Sofi could share the cabin with her, which he allowed, to Sofi's delight. Sara regaled her with imaginative stories of previous inhabitants of the cabin, their peculiarities and their fates. She predicted that the ghost of an Italian princess who had traveled to Spain when she was five years old, just like Sofi, would visit the cabin in the deep of night, while they were sleeping.

"No!" Sofi objected. "Ghosts are dead and they scare me!"

Sara assured her this ghost would smile, be friendly, and have no mean thoughts.

At night, they traced pictures in the starry sky through the porthole before they got under their blankets and were lulled to sleep by the roll of the sea.

The first port of call was Marseilles, where the ship unloaded some cargo and took on two passengers, a Moroccan merchant, Ibrahim, and his young son Omar. They were clothed in white caftans, wore embroidered skull caps, and carried their possessions in valises embellished with Arabic design. They settled into a corner of the steerage reserved for passengers and kept politely to themselves, draping a roll of cloth from the ceiling, to show respect for the privacy of the women. At intervals of the day they bowed and recited prayers of homage to Allah.

When the ship docked at a Balearic island, one the sailors opted to jump ship and run off while the others were loading cargo. He was replaced by Nikos, a beached Greek seaman who beheld Wanda and fell in love.

The first sight of her copper hair and brown eyes inspired tremendous energies in the region of his chest and groin. He muttered, "This woman, I adore her. I worship her. She is a goddess."

Wanda was aware of his passion as he entreated her with suggestive smiles, winks, fervid glances. He sang romantic Greek lyrics aloud and went about with his furry chest bared. He slid by her in passageways with his pelvis rubbing against her behind. At first flattering and somewhat comical, Nikos' attention became a nuisance bordering on an ordeal. She feared Daniel would become aware of them and suspect she was purposely enticing the man.

Late one night she stood alone at the bow, gazing at the moon's reflection on the sea, listening to the rhythm of the waves. Nikos, standing watch, checked to make sure they were alone and sidled close to her. She felt his hands on her shoulders, sliding toward her bosom. Abruptly she pivoted, picked up a bucket of salt water and jammed it on his head. She kneed him in the crotch and he sank painfully to his knees. Before walking off, she pounded noisily on the bucket.

When she returned to Daniel's side, he was sleeping peacefully.

The rest of the voyage, Nikos cast hurt and angry glances at her, but kept his distance.

A goddess, maybe, but crazy in the head.

On the eighteenth day after Genoa, the wind slowed to a whisper, the sea was becalmed, and the skies were ominously gray.

"A storm is brewing," said the captain. "It'll be soon."

The clouds darkened and the humidity became oppressive.

It broke as night fell. Suddenly the wind picked up strength, the temperature cooled, the waves began leaping wildly and a heavy rain commenced to fall. Veins of lightning flashed across the sky and thunder cracked and rumbled like the voice of doom.

The wind got so strong the captain sent men aloft to trim the sails. One lost his footing and fell to the deck, breaking an arm and a cheek bone.

For twenty hours it rained without cease, sheets of water obscuring all creation but their hapless vessel

Water washed over the deck, seeped through cracks and trickled into every corner of the ship.

The passengers huddled in blankets in the darkness, attempting to escape in sleep as the ship rose and fell with the waves.

"Do you think it's the great flood again," whispered Eli," washing away the world's sins?"

"No," said Georgi, "God's just reminding us who's boss."

"Shush," said Anna, "and go to sleep."

In the cabin above, Sara and Sofi slept peacefully as though the storm was but a harmless dream. Sofi turned toward a rag doll and it tumbled softly onto the floor.

The baby moved in sporadic bursts of energy and woke Sara for brief moments.

"So you think the storm is glorious and exciting," she murmured. "Very soon there will be a whole world to play in."

The tumultuous weather cleared as dramatically as it had begun. The sun, with a radiant smile, transformed the gray sky into sparkling blue.

The captain looked up and saw a frigate bird hovering overhead. They were close now. He told the crew to hoist the sails.

They streamed into the harbor of Barcelona the next morning, past the swaying masts of ships waving a colorful array of flags.

The captain crossed himself.

Part Three

SPAIN

He joined the world at an inn in Barcelona under the shadow of the cathedral on May 30th, 1459.

A traveling wine merchant, a wealthy man breathing sour breath, told the proprietor she must turn the foreigners away because the crying of a baby would disturb his sleep.

The proprietor said the foreigners could stay as long as it pleased them and told the merchant he was free to stay or leave. He stayed, petulantly.

Moments after the birth, cathedral bells announced the hour of noon. A shaft of sunlight streamed through the room where mother and infant lay, and illuminated a microcosm of floating dust.

Anna washed the fluid from the infant, dried him, and lifted him for Sara to see. She opened her arms and received him as the bells ceased their mid-day music..

"A boy?" she asked. "Yes, a boy."

"We'll name him after your lost one. How do we say 'Peter' in Spanish?"

"Pedro, I think."

"This is Pedro, then."

After six hours of labor, Sara's face was drawn in exhaustion and there were dark circles under her eyes. Still, she looked radiant. She asked Anna and Wanda to leave the room so she could rest.

Peter blinked his unfocused eyes, emitted a short cry, and slept between his mother's milky breasts.

The men and boys were sitting on the cathedral steps watching people move about in the warm sunlight. Sofi was coddling a stray cat when she saw Anna and Wanda walking toward them.

"Momma!" she cried.

Anna waved.

Daniel rose as they approached. "Well? What?"

"Well guess what, you're a grandfather," said Wanda. "It's a boy, large and healthy." Daniel raised his arms and eyes heavenward.

"Praise be!"

The others repeated it.

Several people paused in their strolls and conversations to regard the odd group of strangers exclaiming excitedly in a foreign tongue. Georgi faced them, cradled his arms and swayed maternally, as though holding an infant.

"Ah, it's a new baby," said a passing woman. Grinning, she mimicked Georgi's pantomime until her husband steered her away.

"When can we see him?" asked Daniel.

"Wait three hours," said Wanda. "She needs rest. We're going back with Sofi now."

"The baby will need a cradle," said Wanda.

"Soon," said Daniel. "Soon I'll buy wood and make a cradle. We have to find somewhere to live and work. Patience, we've been here only a day."

On the street, a group of people formed to begin a Catalonian dance. The males' heads were adorned with stocking caps, the females' with scarves. The young women wore blouses and skirts stitched with elaborate embroidery and the young men were attired in plain white shirts and britches. They mingled awhile, talking, flirting, milling about, until their leader clapped his hands and they formed into a circle, their arms around one another's waists. Slowly, the dancers moved in sidestep to the music of a drum, guitar, and flute. As the tempo increased, they shifted into a forceful heel and toe step, eventually breaking away from the circle to dance as couples, moving close together, then swirling, gliding away and changing partners. It went on like that until the music slowed and they formed into a circle again, sidestepping, holding hands, and ending with bows and curtsies to the audience, which responded enthusiastically with applause and cheers.

Sara, drifting in a realm between wakefulness and sleep, pulled the blanket over Pedro's shoulders and neck. She wondered if the sound of music and cheering had been part of a dream.

In compliance with law, the proprietress notified the Office of Registry there had been a birth at the inn, and the Chief of Registry sent a young clerk named Felipe to record it.

As he walked through the winding streets near the old Roman wall, Felipe was preoccupied with very grave matters—his love for a certain Violeta, whose parents did not regard him highly, and his yen to punish the Chief of Registry for ridiculing the hump on his back. Was that the reason Violeta's father was cool toward him? His malformed back?

Undoubtedly yes, but he, Felipe, knew how to read and write and calculate numbers, and many families would be proud to have such a one in their midst, who might some day rise to eminence in government service. They should consider, too, that he was a skilled swordsman, a man who would defend his family to the death.

Brooding thus, he didn't hear his name called from the tavern. "Felipe!"

He heard it the second time. It was Magda, his father's mistress. "Good day, Magda. I'm on business. I can't stop now."

"Stop, Felipe, for just a moment, and have some wine. Tell me how it goes. What urgent business are you on, that you can't talk to Magda?"

He shrugged indifferently, sat on a bench and watched her pour some wine into a tumbler.

"A foreign woman has given birth at an inn and I must go and record it for the official archives."

"Ah, Felipe, such a significant man you are becoming, clever and astute like your father."

She stroked his head, he brushed her hand off in irritation, and stood abruptly. "I must go now. Thank you for the wine."

"Wait, let me come with you. I'll close this place. Only flies are interested in wine today."

"All right then, but hurry."

At the inn, the proprietress led them to the room where Sara sat singing softly to Pedro and rocking him in her arms.

"Would you tell me, please, your husband's name, your

name, and the name of your baby?"

Sara, not understanding, said something in Polish and then in Yiddish, and it was Felipe's turn to look confused. He asked the proprietress, "What land are these people from?"

"Somewhere in Poland. That's all I know. I can understand their coins but not their words."

Felipe noticed a Torah book on a shelf, opened it and pointed at the Hebrew letters. "Jewish? You are Jewish?"

She comprehended and nodded her head. "Si. Jewish."

"Well that's not difficult," Magda said to Felipe. "We can go to the business of a friend of mine, a converso, and ask him to translate. It's not far."

Felipe kicked some stones along the way. He had a funny feeling about Jews. His father said there was a curse on them because they were not honorable toward Jesus, even though Jesus was himself a Jew. And the ones who became Christians, his father said, you never could be sure if they meant it, or were using it to climb the social ladder and rise above good honest Spaniards. And foremost, his father resented that so many conversos were in important positions, even as advisors to the king and queen.

"Unfortunately, they are smart. They know how to wheedle people to get what they want. And everybody who owns a little property thinks he must have a physician of Jewish background. But don't worry. Their time will come."

Such considerations did not burden Magda. She took people as she found them, with scant regard for malicious tongue wagging.

"The owner of that business." she said, pointing at a

fabric shop, "is an honest man who loaned my cousin money at a fair rate. I think he can help us."

Avranel was a short, lean man of perhaps fifty, with a greying beard. He left off measuring some strips of wool to greet his visitors.

"Good day, Magda. What brings you away from your tavern? Have you come to kindle a romance?"

She laughed. "Not today. Felipe here must record a birth and the family speaks only Yiddish or Polish. Can you help us?"

"Yes, I believe I can. Is it far?"

"No, it's an inn near the cathedral."

At the inn they found Sara sitting up, dressed, except for an exposed breast Pedro was feeding on. Embarrassed, she removed the baby from her nipple and adjusted her bodice. Pedro emitted a whimper at the injustice at this. The other women sat across the room chatting, patching some frayed clothing.

Avranel introduced himself and explained he had come from Lithuania thirty years previously, after his village had been sacked by marauders from God knows where.

"This official, Felipe, has come from the Registry to record the birth of your baby. I will translate the information for him."

After the time, place, and witness details of Pedro's birth were written, Felipe asked the name of the father. Sara hesitated a moment, and said, "Gabriel Stefanek."

"Stefanek. And of course, you and your child Pedro have that same surname."

"Of course."

"And what was his occupation?"

"He was a soldier and he died in battle."

"Heroically, I presume," said Felipe.

He tucked the leather record book under his arm and bowed. He was keenly aware that Sara, though fatigued, was quite beautiful and thought that perhaps they would meet again some day. Who knows what would happen with Violeta and her fence straddling family?

"Well then, this birth of Pedro Stefanek to Sara Stefanek is duly recorded. I hope that you thrive in this great land."

On the street, Magda patted Felipe's back and said, "Bravo."

"There are some important things I need to tell you," Avrel said to Anna and Wanda. "Where are your men?"

"Nearby, at the plaza," said Anna. "Wanda and I can bring you to them. Sofi, you stay here and keep Sara and Pedro company."

They found Georgi and Daniel seated at a stone table, playing a card game. Aron and Eli were at the fringe of a crowd watching a troupe of acrobats juggle, tumble, and form a human pyramid.

Anna introduced Avranel.

"This man is from Lithuania," she said, "and helped to record the birth of Sara's child.

He would like to tell us something important."

"Welcome to Barcelona," he said. "If you're intending to

stay in this city, there are certain things I'd like you to know."

"Yes of course. Please tell us," said Daniel.

"One thing you should know," said Avranel, "is that there are not so many Jews, or rather ex-Jews, who came to Spain from Eastern Europe, as we did. Many arrived from Judea by way of North Africa many hundreds of years ago after our people were scattered by the Romans. These Sephardic ones see themselves as true Spaniards and many of them look down upon our kind as embarrassing distant cousins. But of course, not all are biased or lacking in generosity. You'll find that when you learn the language and are practicing your trades, you'll have a place in this land. But if you want to stay here, you must convert to Christianity or your lives could be in danger."

"Why danger?" asked Georgi.

"About eighty years ago, there were massacres of Jews throughout Spain, and forced conversions. In this city, the Jews who weren't murdered by crazed mobs fled and never returned, or converted to Christianity at the point of a sword. Some committed suicide."

"What would happen if we chose to stay and live openly as Jews?" asked Daniel. "If you tried to do that, sooner or later you might be killed, in the name of God,"

"A God of insanity," said Georgi.

"Yes, but that's the way it is," said Avranel. "My own parents were weary of fleeing hateful pogroms, only to arrive here and find more. So now we are Catholics."

"And now you are safe?" asked Daniel.

"Not completely. Every Jew who ever converted is

suspected of being a backslider and practicing Judaism in secret—a heinous crime in the eyes of the Church. This is also the case with Muslims who have converted. Accused converts have little defense and are often persecuted in ways I don't want to describe."

"I can tell you this." said Daniel, "We're going to hold our heads up and be who we are. Where in this land is that possible?"

"In Verola, after the massacres," said Avranel, "Jews were eventually allowed to resume their identity and religious practices, and are relatively safe, but they must live in a restricted zone known as the Call. They have not been forced to convert and some have more freedom than others. At one time Verola was a center of Jewish scholarship and freedom."

"How far is Verola?" asked Georgi.

"It's northeast, perhaps sixty miles. You could reach it by coach in three days if there were no problems on the road."

Daniel and Georgi exchanged glances and nodded.

"Then that's what we're going to do," said Daniel. "But first my daughter must rest from the strain of giving birth."

"That will be no problem," said Avranel. "The law in Barcelona is that Jews may stay as long as fourteen days before they move on to somewhere else."

"Do you know someone who can take us to Verola?" asked Georgi.

"Near my place of business is a horse corral owned by a friend. He has two coaches and could provide two drivers at a reasonable price. When would you want to go?"

"In five days time," said Daniel. "If that's agreeable to all."

"I'm for it," Georgi said. "And how about you?" he asked Anna and Wanda. They nodded in agreement.

"We don't want to be here if we're despised," said Anna.

A blend of medieval and contemporary architecture surrounded by rivers, hills, and lush foliage, Verola proved to be a more amiable place than they had expected. The stately bell tower of Holy Saints Cathedral loomed high above the city, proclaiming the hours with peals of devotion.

As Jews, the families of Daniel and Georgi were obliged to reside within the "Call," or Juderia. After some deft and exhausting bargaining, and with the agreement of the women, the men purchased a pair of houses on the northern edge of the Call that included a large shop where they could ply their trade. The homes, built around flowered courtyards in the amiable style of Catalonia, had been the inheritance of Juan Da Aragon, a young man whose parents had perished in a shipwreck off the port of Cadiz.

Juan, never comfortable with his identity as a Jew, intended to convert to Catholicism, move to the Christian sector of Verola, and start a new life, perhaps apprentice himself to an engineer and marry a beautiful gentile woman. He had not shared this plan with any relative or acquaintance and it pleased him he would simply be gone, leaving those who knew him to puzzle over his defection.

Several evenings a week, a neighboring widow gave lessons in the Catalan mode of Spanish to the two families, in return for some work the men did on the roof of her house. What had seemed at first a difficult language with its trills and multiple conjugations became gradually more comprehensible, and finally a way to communicate.

Daniel and Aron, not as linguistically adept as the others, found the learning slow going, and were given extra tutoring by Wanda, who had a nimble mind for language. Eli picked it up so easily he was able to serve as interpreter and intermediary in complicated exchanges with the local citizenry. His speech defect was rarely evident any more, and the shame it had brought was but an unpleasant memory.

Daniel and Wanda were formally married at the synagogue two weeks before the high holy day of Atonement in September. During the summer, Wanda had taken instruction, and transitioned gradually from a catholic to a jew. This had been done quietly and secretly, so as to evade the attention of Church spies and local busybodies who might want to make trouble.

She and Anna had been so busy establishing households that they found just a few occasions to quarrel, and mindful of Maria's admonition, kept their disagreements mild. In bed on a Sunday morning, roused by the bark of a garrulous and lonely mongrel,

Daniel confessed to Wanda there were moments when he missed Poland.

"I think of it hardly at all," she said, "and I don't miss it. Here with you, is all I want."

In a different bed in a different house, Anna spoke nostalgically of the river they had left behind.

"Sometimes I think of sitting under that oak by the riverbank, the sway of the reeds, and the fishes making little splashes. Moments that were simple and perfect."

"You know," said Georgi, " all those years as a wandering monk, yearning for some holy revelation, I never found anything more profound than what you just said: 'Simple and perfect.'"

Little Pedro, unlike his mother, had dark eyes and dark hair. It appeared he would blend in plausibly as a Spaniard, and a very large one. It was clear, from the length and breadth of his bones, that he was going to become a very big man. Sara could see the count in his features, but felt no pain in that regard. This was her son Pedro, and the count was the count.

So many doted on him, and fussed over him, that she became watchful lest he become spoiled and demanding. When she decided the adoration was too much she would whisk him away to a quiet place where he could dawdle in peace and solitude. He was content, then, to observe bugs on the wall, attend to the music of birds, and point a finger at magical occurrences known only to himself.

Sofi, five years his senior, was delighted to have a companion so close to the floor.

She regarded him as a jolly doll and they spoke in a secret babble unintelligible to grown-ups. The gibberish he responded with sent her into peals of laughter that he would acknowledge with a crinkled face and a series of wiggles.

In all, Pedro would tell you those were good days, occasionally marred by a bit of gas, or a late feeding, or a cat that drew away. When it was all too much, when the myriad of stimuli tired him, his eyelids would grow heavy, his face would slacken, and his young mother would set him gently in the cradle to drift into the realm of slumber.

The Dominican priest Tomas de Torquemada was considered by his fellow churchmen to be learned, devout, and a model of asceticism. Yet within those ranks were some who felt he was a menace, a man fired with ambition and political acumen, who knew how to sway others and wield personal power. It was expected he would scale the ladder of prestige like his Uncle Juan who had so pleased Pope Eugene IV that he had been made a cardinal.

Already his influence was strong in the royal house of Castile, where he was confessor to young Isabella, half-sister of King Enrique. Close to royal power, Torquemada could, he hoped, make inroads on his primary passion, the weeding out of heretics from the Church. It was said secretly and perhaps spitefully by some skeptical priests, that he was morbid, even maniacal, on the subject of heresy:

"The suspicion of converts secretly practicing Jewish, Muslim, or magic rituals, why does that obsess him so? It could be that deep within, he recoils with self-loathing.

Everyone knows there is Jewish blood in his family."

It was one thing to bandy that sort of gossip about in private, another to say it to his face. Torquemada was simply too powerful and well-connected a man to tangle with.

He behaved toward Isabella as a wise but stern father, guiding her education with a strict adherence to church doctrine and the teachings of Gospel. He asserted that as one who might rule some day, she was obliged to rule foremost as a supporter of Christ, and regard the world as an arena where Satan constantly seeks to undermine the Kingdom of Heaven.

Armando, a young priest assigned to serve as his aide, was invariably uncomfortable in Torquemada's presence. He would get tongue-tied and make foolish mistakes. He begged the bishop to assign him elsewhere, perhaps to a small village where he would serve people who were plain and simple like himself.

"There is much you can learn from Fray Tomas de Torquemada," the bishop said, "but little you can learn in the countryside that you don't already know. If you are having difficulty, see it as a test of your strength and overcome it."

Years later, Armando would relate to a friend that the bishop had been right, there had been much to learn from Torquemada.

"If anything, I learned that moderation and humility are high virtues and were totally lacking in this man. I learned that personal power can lead to the delusion one is acting as God's divine instrument where one is in fact acting in his own self-interest. There are times I would hate Torquemada, times I would pity him or fear him, but never once was I able to feel any real affection for him, and do you know what unsettles me? I tried to emulate him in various ways. In spite of myself, I was prompted by his example to change my behavior. God forgive me, but I began to give absolutist sermons as though I had a pipeline to heaven. I preached intolerance for weaknesses of the flesh that I myself couldn't overcome. I lived ascetically in a barren room and ate plain food until I was bursting with spiritual pride as though I were a candidate for sainthood.

"What finally freed me from the man, paradoxically, was love, or a distortion of love. I happened upon him teaching Isabella one morning. She was wearing a white gown, and looking, I must say, quite pretty. He was regarding her with admiration. While she was reading aloud, he reached over and touched her shoulder and he gently stroked her hair. Somehow, he sensed my presence, removed his hand, swiveled around and saw me standing there looking foolish with a document in my hand. He flushed, his deep-set eyes were burning, his features were contorted in anger and discomfort. 'What do you want?' he shouted."

"I handed him the bishop's missive, excused myself and left. In a matter of days, I received a notice I was assigned to a church in the north. That was the last I ever saw of him, praise the Lord."

Torquemada was not physically imposing until one looked into his eyes. He had a powerful gaze that could hold people in sway so that later they would recall looking at him but not recall what he had said. It was common for people to look away when talking with him.

His fervent hope for Spain was that someday the kingdoms of Aragon and Castile would unite to form one Catholic country and purge itself of Judaism, Islam, and divergent forms of Christianity. He yearned for the time when the land would be a light unto the world, a place where Christ's mission was in full flower, eternally witnessed by the True Church and shepherded by himself, Tomas de Torquemada.

He was a man who knew who he was and what had to be done. He had no patience with bumblers who got in the way.

Wanda told Sara the young doctor Jacobo Olavide had approached Daniel for permission to call on her at the house and Daniel had consented.

"Jacobo Olavide?" Sara raised her eyes in mock consternation. "He looks like a scarecrow. He has orange hair like straw and flaps his arms when he talks. And when he talks to me he mixes his Catalan and Ladino into such a Spanish goulash that I hardly know what he's saying."

"Well, tell him to stick with the Catalan, then. He wouldn't be such a bad match, you know. His family is well connected and he has a bright future as a physician. Such husbands are not easy to come by."

"Would you want Jacobo Olavide for a husband?"

"What a question!" said Wanda. "How would I know? Maybe I would, under different circumstances. Maybe not. To be honest, my preference goes in a different direction. Daniel is just right."

Sara felt a flash of anger. At times she thought of her departed mother and felt a tinge of resentment toward Wanda, as though she were an interloper. She knew that wasn't reasonable, but still it came.

The idea of a husband wasn't very compelling, though she knew it would be beneficial to have someone to care for her and Pedro, and take the burden off Daniel. Such an odd, unexpected prospect, and yet, he was a suitor. Perhaps if she got to know him.

She was secretly in love with Gabriel, the phantom father of Pedro, the swain who never existed. The intriguing thing about Gabriel, in her imagination, was that he wasn't constant. He changed form and mood like the weather, or some demigod who appeared in various guises for various reasons. Currently, he was dark-haired, a trifle pale, and utterly selfish. He took her as he wanted, cruelly, and kept his gentler side from view. When they lay together his eyes would scrutinize her as though to say, "Who, really, are you?" and the query would drive her past reason to a calm dark oblivion.

Jacobo had appeared in her life a year before, to examine Pedro after a fall had bruised his cheek and jaw and blackened an eye. Pedro, then thirteen months old, had been crawling across a table following the progress of a shiny doodlebug when the table ended and he found himself on the floor. That was a fascinating situation for a moment, until the floor taught him a painful lesson about gravity. Sara, hearing the thump and subsequent yowls, gathered him up, and fearing breakage, carried him to the clinic of Dr. Jacobo Olavide.

Gentle probing yielded a quick diagnosis.

"Sound! Absolutely fine! No cracks or breaks, and I can see by the symmetry in his eyes that there are no internal injuries. My advice is, take him home, feed him, and let him go to sleep. When he awakens, you can relieve the swelling with a cool, damp cloth."

Pedro, on the examining table, watched the doctor's excited gestures with fascination.

Particularly interesting was the man's orange hair that jumped as he talked, and was given a halo by the light from the window. He pointed a finger at the lively thatch, said something in gibberish and formed a bruise-faced grin.

Jacobo recommended she bring the infant for general health checkups every four months, and compensate him by making window curtains for his clinic, if she liked.

He watched the sway of her hips as he left.

"I don't think she knows how sensual she really is," he confided to an ivory skull on his desk. "Strong, intelligent, and mysterious, too."

Jacobo was a hybrid, the offspring of a Sephardic Jewish father and a Catholic mother whose family had emigrated from Brandenburg after an aborted peasant uprising. At his mother's insistence, Jacobo had been baptized in her faith, and later, at his father's insistence, underwent Hebrew instruction at a local shul. He resolved that paradox by placing his faith in science and cultivating a bored indifference toward all houses of worship. It amused him that he could, when he wanted, go from Jew to Christian as easily as a chameleon went from green to brown.

When he decided to woo Sara he knew it would portend a Jewish wedding to satisfy her family, and he was at peace with that, though he realized it would be a strain on his mother.

"Catalan Spanish, just Catalan, please," said Sara. "And

not too fast. There are still words I don't know."

They were strolling along the waterfront on a balmy afternoon when his clinic duties had been few. He bought them orange juice from a vendor and led Sara to a shaded table where they could watch the bustle of boats docking and leaving, and passengers chattering excitedly.

"Why did you want to call on me?"

"The thing is, Sara, I thought you were an interesting person. I thought perhaps we could get acquainted. Who knows. There may, some day, develop a sympathy between us."

As they talked, Sara found that Jacobo's animated manner was not so ludicrous, but fueled by spontaneity, and she perceived his mind worked in a unique way, spawning a myriad of ideas.

When a passing deckhand leered at her and uttered an improper remark, Jacobo sprang to his feet and rebuked him.

"Watch your manners and keep to your work." The man glared sullenly, and kept moving.

"Tell me about your husband," said Jacobo. "What was he like?"

She didn't answer. They resumed walking for a while, attending to the clacking of their footsteps on cobblestones.

"I'll tell you but not right now."

"All right."

The following week he sat with her family at a Sabbath meal prepared by Wanda and Sara well before sundown so that God wouldn't catch them tardy. They ate tranquilly as was Sabbath custom, avoiding extraneous, aggravated talking. At a previous dinner in what now seemed a bygone world, Rabbi Kline had said light and silence were the Lord's favorite dwelling places, hence the custom of lighting candles and speaking with calm restraint on the seventh day.

After the meal, Jacobo and Sara joined Georgi's family for a stroll up a hill, eventually slipping away to perch on a log and watch a group of children cavorting around a bonfire far below. Their excited voices leapt into the air with the flames and the streams of smoke. An aroma of burning cedar chips mingled agreeably with the evening breeze.

"You wanted to know about my husband," said Sara. "I might as well tell you."

She described first the village where she was raised, imparting a sense of life in a place where the inhabitants thought and behaved very much alike.

"We all had our roles, nobody questioned them. When Georgi came along, and then a war came along, things changed. It was wonderful and it was also terrible because some people were so upset they acted mean and crazy."

"The ordeal of change," said Jacobo. "Excuse me, please go on."

"Now that I look back I can see that everything was always changing but we didn't realize it."

"'A million changes are but a moment in the mind of God.' That's from a Sufi poet."

"Sorry, no more interruptions."

"Well, it was the little war that changed things forever. Our men were marched off to kill and die for the sport of a few noblemen. When they came back they were different— sad and lost in a way. They brought some of our neighbors and relatives back in coffins, and they had wounds in their spirits. You could see it in their eyes, and the way they acted.

"But that changed too. Time heals all wounds, as they say, and life in the village gradually got more normal. Then one normal spring day I went for a walk in the woods. I was sitting by a creek with my feet in the water, just happy to be alive."

She paused and was quiet for a few moments, gazing at the bonfire. "I don't want to talk about it but I will, I want you to know the rest."

She told about the count appearing, her fear, and how one thing led to another, until she was pinned under the weight of his large body.

"It was like being awake and in a bad dream at the same time."

She glanced at Jacobo to gauge his reaction. He met her eyes calmly, with comprehension.

"There was nothing I could do about it."

"Of course not. You have nothing to blame yourself for. Not a thing."

"Anyway, Pedro came from it and I'm glad to have him."

They sat a while longer, and got up to join the others at the crest of the hill. A lizard scurried out of their path into the safety of a clump of rocks. Cautiously, it peeked its head out to watch them leave.

"But tell me," said Jacobo, "how did you decide on 'Gabriel' as the father's name?"

"I don't know. It just came to mind."

Jacobo felt a glow travel from his chest throughout his body. He craved to lift her up and carry her up the hill. He wondered if the story of the count had enhanced his affection for her in a way that was perverse. He decided he would ask for her hand in marriage at their next meeting.

Daniel gave his blessing to the wedding with a jocular but pointed admonition: "You must remember, if you are not good to our little Sara, you may end up with lumps on your head."

"You can be at peace on that score," said Jacobo. "It would be easier for me to cut off my nose than to treat her badly."

His own parents had hoped to see him marry into a wealthy well-placed family, but were reconciled to have Sara as a daughter-in-law. After a friendly drinking bout with Daniel, Arturo Olavide came home to the blurry form of his wife Greta and told her, drunkenly, that her son had made an excellent choice, and that she should not try to make trouble with her sharp tongue. She called him an idiot and a drunken sot and stomped out of the room.

"They're getting married by a rabbi!" she shrieked from the bedroom. "She's not a virgin!"

"Be quiet!" shouted Arturo. "Be quiet!" He hurled a boot at the bedroom door and curled up on the floor to sleep.

When Greta met the family it was Pedro with his bright swarthiness and personable ways who melted her resistance. He climbed onto her lap, touched her face, and said enigmatically, "Cloud."

A grandson of sorts, ready made. She thought it might be pleasant to bake confections for this little person, and shop for gifts. She had to concede Sara was a graceful young woman and seemed capable of being a good wife to Jacobo, though only time could tell.

The newlyweds moved into a house not far from Jacobo's practice that gave an easterly view of the river and was within reasonable walking distance of Sara's family and friends.

The wedding ceremony had been conducted in Ladino, giving it an elegant, cryptic quality, in the assessment of the celebrants on the Polish side. The nuptial canopy had fluttered gently in the breeze and attracted the attention of some gulls that circled down to see what could be pilfered. The August sun was hot, radiating waves that evoked a mirage-like shimmer on the distant horizon. Crawling, hopping, and winged insects sported cheerfully on the grass, hedges, and flowers.

The betrothed, remarkably attired in silk, vowed to love and honor in a ritual that harkened to societies before recorded time.

Aron vowed he wouldn't weep, as the others were doing. What a sight, Georgi, Anna, Wanda, Eli, all of them weeping sentimentally. Even his father, big sturdy Daniel, had tears streaking down his cheeks and was making sobbing noises. What in hell were they crying about? It was supposed to be a happy occasion, his sister's wedding. It was true of course that she looked hauntingly beautiful, and it seemed like some infinite grace had descended, but that was no reason to blubber. Circumspectly, Aron turned to the side, lifted a sleeve and dried the tears from his face.

After the ceremony, relatives and friends flocked around the banquet table, introduced themselves, made an effort to socialize with those they didn't know.

Several middle-aged women voiced regret as they munched, that their own daughters, flowers of Sephardim, had not been matched with the young doctor and his prestigious family. But such banalities were drowned in the gaiety of wine, music and toasts.

"Today," Daniel boomed, "it's no sin to drink your fill and love your neighbors."

"Unless it's your neighbor's wife," amended Arturo.

"Even that!" Daniel seized Greta in a bear hug and raised her high. She shrieked in laughter, blushing, punching at his shoulders.

Pedro drank some sherry from a neglected goblet and found intoxication to his liking.

He ran about in high spirits until the heat and excitement exhausted his two-year-old body. As guests began to leave, Sara asked, in alarm, where Pedro was. A furious search turned him up under the shade of a bush, his chin spattered with Manzanilla. "Ah, well," said Georgi, "how many children get to be present at their mother's wedding?"

They called the king of Castile "Enrique the Impotent" because he couldn't control his kingdom or beget a royal heir. The land was disordered with civil war, fields were abandoned by fleeing peasants, the roads were unsafe for commerce. Nobles carried on vengeances against one another in a series of sieges and conspiracies that seemed endless. Currency was deflated as were the spirits of the people in1463, the year Jacobo brought his family to live in the palace at Segovia.

"Judging from the gossip I've heard these last two days, Aragon is a model of sane and stable government compared to this kingdom," said Jacobo.

"Well then, let's go back."

He looked to see if Sara was joking. She smiled impishly and they broke into laughter.

The situation they were in suddenly struck them as wildly absurd and their laughter was a relief from fatigue and tension.

Two months before, an envoy from the court of Castile had appeared at Jacobo's clinic with an offer of one thousand doblas if he would move his practice to Segovia. Jacobo had pondered whether the man was insane, like one of those people who claimed to be Julius Caesar, or Moses, or some other grandiose figure. He was grave and secretive to the point of melodrama.

"Look here, I don't know you and I've never been to Segovia. This is outlandish, very hard to believe. Why would you make such an offer?"

"It was my task," said Luis, the envoy, "to find a physician outside of Castile with impeccable skill and reputation. I inquired around Verola and your name came up several times. I've watched you and I've talked to some of your patients.

I'm convinced you're the right man."

"You've been spying on me."

"I wouldn't put it that way. I've been gathering impressions."

Jacobo pondered whether to send him away and put an end to such nonsense. "Let me see an official document and let me see some of that money."

Luis unraveled a small scroll and placed it on the table. It identified him as a special emissary of Enrique IV, King of Castile, and bore an official stamp and the apparent signature of the king. He reached into his valise, removed a leather pouch, loosened a drawstring, and a hundred coins spilled onto the table.

"This is yours, if you want it. I'll give you two hundred more before you leave Verola, and there are seven hundred waiting for you when you reach Segovia. At the end of your tenure you will receive one hundred more as a bonus of appreciation. I have these assurances for you in writing. What do you say?"

Jacobo said nothing, for a while. A thousand doblas was more of a fortune than he would amass in a lifetime.

"You'll have to explain," he said.

"Very well. I am a cousin of the Marques of Villena, and from time to time I represent the King of Castile as an agent in delicate matters. The king has a daughter whom he claims he begot, who would, in the natural course of events, succeed him to the throne. His detractors, of whom there are many, claim that Enrique could not have sired Juana because he is impotent with women and prefers to dally with men. They say the child's mother, Juana of Portugal, has been so wanton with men at court that young Juana could have been spawned by any number of them including even the captain of the guard.

"What do you think?" asked Jacobo."

"To be honest, the king is a poof, and I am one of those who doubt he fathered Juana. But who can say? Who can prove he didn't roll onto the queen one night, poke an erection into her and squirt the fluid that formed a daughter?"

"If no one can prove otherwise, then what is the problem?"

"The problem is that nobody believes it."

Luis explained the custom in Castile of there being witnesses and a notary at the bedside of the king and queen on the wedding night. In neither of Enrique's two marriages was he able to rise to the occasion. In the case of Juana, the present queen, he claimed paternity of her child, and no one challenged it.

"The kingdom of Castile is floundering in turmoil," said Luis. "There are many who despise Enrique and would wrest the crown from him and settle it on his half-brother Alfonso."

Jacobo wasn't sure that would be such a bad thing, but then, the quagmire of political falderal was beyond his experience and reckoning. It also occurred to him that performing before an audience on one's wedding night could be unnerving for any man.

"And what would be my role in all this? Why am I worth a thousand doblas?"

"For that sum you will serve as physician to the young Princess Juana and watch over her health like a mother hen.

The king, not unreasonably, fears there is a conspiracy in the land to poison the child. He doesn't trust that there is any doctor in Castile who would withstand offers of power and money to join in a death plot."

"But you don't know if I would be reliable either."

"It is my judgment that you are. If I am mistaken I could forfeit my life."

"Let me think about this and discuss it with my wife."

"Agreed."

"If I were to take the position it would be for no more than four years."

"That's acceptable. You could then enter a new agreement or return to Verola." Strolling along the river's edge that night, Luis encountered a most appealing Frenchwoman attired in a red dress. Before they fornicated, he kissed the brunette triangle between her legs. Afterward, before falling asleep, he felt the self-disgust that came after being with a whore. Whores excited him more than other women, but there was always the remorse.

Sara, Jacobo, and Pedro got out of the carriage, stretched their limbs, and beheld their new residence with awe. Sided by two rivers, the Alcazar, the royal palace at Segovia, jutted out majestically like the prow of a ship.

"My God," said Sara, "Are we walking in a dream?"

Jacobo recognized Luis walking toward them. Beside him was a tall, stooped man with a large head and an angular nose. The latter person spread his arms and said, "Welcome to Segovia."

"This is Enrique IV, King of Castile. It is appropriate to bow," said Luis.

"Never mind, never mind," said the king. "Consider the bows done." He patted Pedro's head and said, "Who have we here? The young Count of Verola?"

Jacobo took a deep breath to calm his racing heart.

"This is Sara, my wife, Pedro my stepson, and I am Dr. Jacobo Olavide, at your service."

"Well then, come into the castle," said the king. "Luis will take you to your chamber. This evening we will dine together, if you would be so kind."

"Farewell, senor the king," said Pedro.

Enrique raised his head and laughed. "How old is he?"

"Six," said Sara.

"He has the makings of a noble. We shall see. We shall see."

As Enrique walked off, Jacobo noted he had a peculiarly unsteady stride, like someone moving through a rambunctious mob. He stopped by a soldier standing guard, put a hand on his shoulder and whispered something that made the soldier laugh.

"Please follow me, and I will take you to your living quarters," said Luis.

In the entryway, they found it somewhat confusing to be standing in the midst of such elegance after the tedious carriage ride. The long foyer was appointed with marble floors, tapestries, stone and oak walls, scarlet drapes, Greco-Roman statues.

"I think Pedro will like this next room," said Luis.

He led them into the Hall of Pineapples. Four hundred gleaming stalactites in the form of golden pineapples hung from the ceiling. Luis smiled to see the family gaping in astonishment.

"Incredible!" Jacobo exclaimed.

"Believe it or not, you can get used to these celestial fruits," said Luis. "People who live here walk through this hall without even looking up."

He led them next into a high-domed gallery, the Room of the Kings.

"Here you have a sense of our history. This project was conceived and supervised by Enrique himself. It is our greatest marvel."

Thirty-four enthroned statues of kings, the lineage of Castile, were gazing calmly into eternity. Their visages, artfully ennobled, bestowed an aura of hushed dignity on the room. The gleaming luster of gilt and polychrome gave an impression of solid gold, indeed many visitors believed that it was.

It occurred to Jacobo that each of these idealized beings had embodied every human quality from ignorance to genius and each in his turn had partaken of the inevitable griefs—disease, madness, loneliness, despair, a loss of loved ones. How many, he wondered, had wearied of their lot as kings and gone gratefully into the sleep of death?

They entered Enrique's throne room with its domed ceiling and elaborate arabesque designs.

"And this, as you see, is where our monarch holds sway. Here, he receives visitors from other kingdoms, reigns at ceremonies, issues edicts, enjoys the art of musicians, poets and acrobats. It is not here but in his library, that he meets with ministers and advisors to discuss the complex matters of ruling a kingdom. You will eventually meet those people and form your own opinions."

A young woman scrubbing the floor waved at Luis. "Hello Rosa," he said.

"That girl is deficient in her intelligence, but always cheerful. Enrique has charged that any man who molests her or uses her badly will be punished severely."

Sara hung back a few moments to watch the girl scrub as the others moved down the hall. The girl put down her brush and smiled. Sara waved and turned to catch up with the others.

"The last place on our tour is yours."

Luiis led them into a large room adorned with velvet drapes, Moorish carpets, elegantly carved furniture, a cano-pied bed. A spacious alcove had been sectioned off with a wall and door and furnished with shelves, a bed, table and chest, to serve as Pedro's private lair.

"Here are the servants with your belongings. I'll leave you to settle in. In four hours you will be summoned to dine with the king and his family."

From the patio, Pedro watched a group of boys playing tag on the lawn in the garden below. The runner attempted to zigzag through a gauntlet without being touched, which rarely happened. After he was tagged he joined the gauntlet and a new runner sprinted through, soon suffering the fate of the previous one.

"Can I go down there?" Pedro asked.

"It looks harmless enough," said Jacobo.

"We just arrived here," said Sara. "We don't know what we can do and what we can't do."

"That's true but we're not prisoners, and we can see Pedro from the balcony. We mustn't get into the habit of being afraid."

"You're right," said Sara. "You can go," she told Pedro, "but only to the garden, nowhere else."

Pedro ran out of the room as servants were bringing in the trunks. In the garden, he walked slowly toward the gauntlet. One of the larger boys called to him.

"Who are you?"

"Pedro."

"Let's see you run."

He was halfway through the gauntlet when one of the boys stepped out of position and shoved him down. Another boy yelled "cheater!" and pushed the shover. The ensuing scuffle was broken up by Manuel, a brawny gardener who clearly had the boys' respect.

"All right boys, all right. Get back in line and play fair."

Sara had been watching anxiously and whispered, "Thank you," when the gardener interceded.

She flopped down on the bed, closed her eyes and listened to the excited shouting of the boys.

"We have privacy," said Jacobo. "Yes."

She took off her dress. They made love.

Thus released, they napped.

What must have seemed ordinary to the hosts was opulent to the guests—venison, lamb, quail, fresh warm bread, vegetables, fruit, pastries, wine.

Pedro was intrigued that the table legs had clawed feet like those of a wild beast. He ducked his head under the table to contemplate the feral wooden feet and the fancy slippers of their royal hosts.

"Sit up," Sara said, and gave him a light cuff. This brought a giggle from little Juana, seated across from him.

At the table with them were Enrique the King, Queen Juana, Juana the presumptive princess, and Don Beltran, Duke of Albuquerque, who was reputed to be the queen's lover and the actual father of young Juana. He had been elevated from mediocrity to dukedom by Enrique, who had found him handsome and dashing. It was not unheard of for the king to settle largesse on young men who pleased him.

Jacobo and Sara appreciated the way wine helped their conversation flow smoothly after they had been feeling strange and shy.

"So, please, doctor, give us your political impressions of Verola and the region of Catalonia. Much of what I know about it is based on rumor, gossip and slander."

"Well perhaps you'll forgive me, your majesty, if I become philosophical. It is my natural inclination to surmise and speculate."

"Please speak freely, doctor. You're my honored guest."

"I think that first off, there is fear. People fear those who are not like them. They reason that if others do not think and behave like them there must be something wrong with them. And so they feel threatened by these others. These others have different religions, different customs, different languages, different communities. They even have the effrontery to look different."

Jacobo paused to estimate the measure of what was allowable before this king, and continued.

"And each individual in his lonely terror perceives himself as an entity that must be protected from outside impingements. To do this he summons hatred to be his army. Hatred can justify. It can strike out. It can destroy that which is feared. Just as individuals have their armies of hatred, so do regions."

A priest entered the room and slid into a seat at the end of the table. Enrique circled his table knife in the air and pointed it at him.

"This is Fray Tomas de Torquemada," he said.

The priest waved a hand wanly in the direction of the guests.

"Our new physician Dr. Olavide, his wife Sara, and his son Pedro."

"Honored," said Torquemada. "Your ideas are very interesting. Please continue."

Jacobo observed the dour cast of the priest's countenance and thought it might be reckless to speculate further, but went on.

"You asked about Catalonian politics. It's a mirror of all the world. In my native city, Verola, people distrust those who live in different neighborhoods, different cities, different regions. Walk by taverns, what do you hear? 'Down with Tarragona, down with Aragon, down with Castile, down with France.' Stated, simply, the political aspirations of Catalonia are comparable to those of any other entity. It would, if it could, secede from Aragon and defeat that country. It would defeat Castile, Leon, Navarre, Granada, rule all of Hispania, rule the whole world, and rule, ultimately, the entire universe."

Enrique burst out laughing.

"The entire universe!" he chortled. "What madness! What divine, silly madness!" The king's infectious laughter spread to others at the table, including the children.

Laughter echoed off the walls, filled the room, rattled the quail bones.

Jacobo noted that Torquemada wasn't laughing.

Guiding young Juana's health, as he had been hired to do, did not take up much of Jacobo's time. The girl had no physical problems, was intelligent, and appeared to be emotionally sound. It was clear he was there for the peace of mind of Enrique, who seemed to trust him.

His duties eventually expanded to anyone in the court who had an ache or pain, including the king and queen. He was astonished at the number of royal attendants who had venereal complaints—itches, sores, swelling, discharges, bladder ailments. He gave them herbal remedies, bone powder pills, and various experimental potions he thought might be helpful. One noble was so ravaged by syphilis that Jcobo decided to treat him with mercury though it could have treacherous side effects. A favorite professor had assured him there was no blame in employing risky remedies in the late stage of a ravaging disease.

He advised the venereal patients to stay clean and dry and abstain from copulation until the symptoms were gone, advice that he knew would be taken lightly. The palace was a honeycomb of complicated sexual intrigues that led to jealousies, beatings, duels, ongoing blood feuds.

"A stiff prick has no conscience, doctor," was the trenchant wisdom of a palace guard treated for a stab wound inflicted by a jealous husband.

Men would make romantic overtures to Sara from time to time and she would demure gracefully. Jacobo knew she wouldn't get drawn into the Alcazar's florid deceits but he was often disgusted with the situation they were in, and the arrogant gall of the men who prodded her.

"No one guaranteed life would be easy," he reminded himself when he reviewed the swirl of events that had brought them to the palace, and longed for the relative simplicity of their lives in Verola.

Pedro in his seventh year had grown so large he was allowed into the playmate realm of boys age eight and upwards. He had shown himself stalwart in a couple of shoving matches, which established his right to participate in the war games the boys played tirelessly, sometimes into the night.

A palace carpenter the war minister had designated

"Deputy of Young Armament" had the task of keeping the boys supplied with wooden staves. Monthly, that minister was impresario of a lavish battle staged for the court and its guests at a clearing the king had dubbed Armageddon.

The boys were divided into Moors and Castilians. Before battle they stood in formation and saluted the assembled guests as a snare drummer beat out a perky cadence. The Moors were costumed with yellow headbands and the Castilians wore blue sashes around their waists. They were assigned sides by lot so there would be no onus attached to portraying an alien Moor, and to ensure a random smattering of ability.

God was formally evoked to sponsor the valor of each side. A priest blessed the Castilians in the name of the Father the Son and the Holy Ghost, followed by the Moors prostrating themselves ostensibly toward Mecca as their leader proclaimed, "There is no God but Allah and Mohammed is his prophet."

Torquemada had complained about the Muslim benediction, averring it should not be uttered in a Christian setting but Enrique overruled him in the interest of drama.

Pedro participated in the first of these mock battles on the side of the Moors. Sara was seated next to Queen Juana who had taken a shine to her. The queen noticed Sara was frowning worriedly,

"You don't have to worry," Juana said. "The boys don't often get hurt. They're trained to slap with only the flats of their swords and they're not allowed to aim for faces."

Jacobo, standing next to Luis, Don Beltran, and the royal bursar, was caught up in the general excitement and keen to see the battle get underway. He was surprised at the level of enthusiasm he felt for a sport that glorified the horror of war and he recognized he must have the same violent potential within himself as any other man.

He overheard the Marques of Villena mutter to another noble, "It's too bad Enrique doesn't have the balls for anything but a make-believe campaign against the Moors."

"Well, don't forget he marched on Granada."

"And don't forget he turned around and marched right back again." They laughed derisively at this.

The war minister waved his arms and the foes moved into position. The Castilians formed two ranks with a space of about ten yards between them, facing a woods where the Moors were deployed between bushes and trees. The bright yellow headbands of the Moors belied their attempt to blend in with the foliage.

With the stage set and the actors poised, the war minister faced the spectators and announced:

"The wily Moors are about to swarm from the woods and attack the Castilians. The Castilians are prepared to stand their ground and defeat the savage unbelievers."

He bowed to the king who rose and proclaimed, "Let it begin!" A trumpet sounded and it began.

The Moors ran out of the woods screaming in high-pitched voices, brandishing their curved scimitars. When they reached the clearing, the spectators applauded and yelled excitedly.

The captain of the Castilians, Alfonso, the king's pubescent half-brother, exhorted his troops, "Hold fast! Don't break the line!"

Jacobo observed that some of the combatants registered fear just as they would in actual warfare.

As the Moors closed in, the first line of defense sprang forward and engaged them in combat. The second line broke ranks and joined the melee despite Alfonso's orders.

Four palace guards acting as referees mingled in the ranks and tagged boys they judged to be dead or wounded. The tagged ones fell to the ground, some of them dramatically clutching at their wounds. Pedro, one of the first to be tagged, rolled out of the way of the rambunctious legs and contemplated the struggle from the ground up. He saw Jaime, a close friend, get slapped on the chest and ruled out. He scanned the spectator area and saw his mother seated by the queen, looking at him with concern.

He got to his knees and waved. She stood and waved back energetically. "Momma," he murmured.

The only serious damage resulted from a fist fight between a Moor and a Castilian over a long-term grudge not related to the spurious battle. The Castilian ended up with a bloody nose and was ruled dead.

The combat was concluded by a blast from the trumpet. The foes regrouped on their respective sides while the minister of war counted the dead and wounded. When the tally was done he addressed the audience:

"His majesty's troops have held the line against the abominable Moors. The Moors suffered twice as many casualties as the Castilians."

The spectators cheered and clapped except for some

parents of the hapless Moors.

The queen held out a bowl of sweets to be distributed among winners and losers alike.

"Tell me Luis," asked Jacobo, "do the Moors ever win?"

"Never."

"My dear mother and father," Jacobo wrote, "since my last letter so much has changed here that it challenges my meager ability to narrate.

"Enrique, whom you know they call 'Enrique the Impotent' has been rendered ever weaker by a rebellion of his grandees and some of his clergy. There has been so much conspiracy, betrayal and counterfoil that it would fill a volume titled, perhaps, Outrageous Schemes in the Kingdom of Castile.

"Sara and Pedro by the way, are quite well, and are looking forward to our return to Verola, which will be soon.

"Let me try to depict the amazing series of events that has crested in these last months.

"A gathering of grandees at Burgos drafted a list of demands, chief among them a demand that Enrique repudiate the fantasy that Juana is his blood daughter and concede that his half-brother Alfonso is rightful heir to the throne. Their document condemns Enrique for mismanaging the kingdom and condemns even his personal morals. It instructs him to acknowledge all charges and repent. It requires him to dismiss his Moorish bodyguard who they say has committed unspeakable lascivious acts upon men and women alike. And it states that the king's beloved Don Beltran must be stripped of his position of power, with the Mastership of Santiago being transferred from Beltran to Alfonso.

"In short, dear parents, the grandees have declared that Enrique has made a mess of things and must clean it up at their command.

"To illustrate the general disgust with Enrique's rule and the smarting pride of Castilian men, I'll tell you of one Paco, a trader who traveled to Aragon last month to buy horses.

"On the way to Teruel, Paco and his companions stopped at two inns for lodging where King Enrique was the subject of hilarity and ridicule among the Aragonese customers. He was called 'Enrique the Fairy King' and all manner of names contemptuous of his manhood. At both inns Paco and cohorts argued and fought to defend the honor of Castile. At the second, one of them was stabbed, and Paco suffered a broken nose. Rather than contend with more of that, they camped on the ground for the rest of the trip.

"At Teruel Paco bought a dozen fine horses from a rancher who invited him and his men to spend the night in a vacant barn. When they prepared to leave in the morning, they found someone had tied a dress and ribbons on one of their newly acquired stallions and attached a sign reading, 'Enrique the Impotent.' Paco removed the attire, his men cinched the horses, and they rode off in humiliation as the rancher and his men laughed raucously.

"Such stories are common and have contributed to a seething resentment of Enrique in a land where pride and honor take precedence over everything.

"But let me try to explain to you the rest of the complicated events that have led to our happy release from the king's service.

"After Enrique caved in and signed the document called the Representation of Burgos, he changed his mind, reinstated Don Beltran, and together they raised a large army to maintain control of the kingdom. The nobles of Burgos, Toledo, Seville, Cordoba, were not impressed. At Avila they deposed Enrique in effigy, tearing off his sword and sceptre and kicking his naked dummy repeatedly. They seated young Alfonso on the throne and declared him king, even kissing his hand.

"Enrique and his army set out to do battle with the nobles at a strategic junction of two rivers, when the situation suddenly changed. The Marques of Villena, a prime mover of the rebellion, betrayed the rebels and brought his troops over to the king's side.

"The battle was called off. Enrique agreed to give his half-sister Isabella in marriage to Pedro Giron, the Master of Calatrava, in return for Villena's fealty, which would mean that Giron would stand close to becoming King of Castile.

"Are you tiring of this tangled web of intrigue and chicanery? Patience, and I'll draw it together as well as I can.

"When Isabella, a pleasant girl of fourteen, learned she had been bartered in marriage to Giron, she was horrified. She came into our quarters in tears and said she was going to flee to Avila (where her mother went insane) and live with the nuns. Sara comforted her as well as she could but the girl was extremely distraught and not unreasonably so, because from

what I hear, the Master of Calatrava was no prize. He was no-
torious as a debauchee, a demonic manipulator of power, and
an ill-tempered boor. Further, he was well into middle age.

"Isabella prayed for deliverance and her prayers were
answered. Don Pedro Giron choked to death of an uncertain
cause on his way to claim Isabella as his bride.

"Without the support of Villena and Giron, it is but a
matter of time before Enrique's kingdom crumbles away
from him entirely. He falls into depression and spends much
of his time in solitude and apathy. He ordered us away (God
be praised) at the nudge of Torquemada after a conversation
between the priest and myself wherein Torquemada asked if
I was a converso. I told him I was not, without mentioning
my baptism. He then asked if I was a believing Jew. I told him
I was, which is not particularly true, as you know. He gave me
a most insolent look and went away. In the evening, Enrique
summoned me to tell me that if my family didn't convert to
the Holy Church we would have to leave in a month's time.
The king's facial tic was pulsating, his eyes were bloodshot,
his color mealy. I suspect he may be going mad.

"At Torquemada's urging the king had signed an edict
that all court Jews must convert to Christianity or leave the
royal service. That is why our background suddenly became
such an issue, though the edict was not necessary. Aside
from us, all court functionaries of Jewish extraction had
converted long ago, even generations ago.

"We're very happy to be leaving this roost of vultures.
You can expect us sometime next month. Please give this
letter to Sara's family and tell them that she and Pedro and I

are well and send our love.

"I remain your affectionate son. "Jacobo."

F. Morales, an exporter of religious artifacts devised a way to avoid paying Ramon Levi a large sum he owed him. At the same time he would set in motion a calamity for the Jewish community, whom he held responsible for his broken dreams. His only son had eloped with a Jewess and gone off to Portugal.

He got into the cathedral's storage room with a stolen key and smeared chicken blood on the eucharist wafers. Next morning, he entered for mass and found the priests in a state of shock and dismay, as he had expected.

"What is it?"

"This!" A priest pointed to the bloody wafers.

"Mother of God!" exclaimed Morales. "Do you know that one of my workers saw a certain Ramon Levi and two other Jews come out of this building late last night?"

"Jews!" shouted the priest. "Jews! They've desecrated the host." As worshipers entered the cathedral, the cry went up.

"Jews! They've contaminated the Host!" A priest held up the evidence.

"See here! The Lord's offering has been violated."

As worshippers crossed themselves, a call for revenge rippled through the crowd. Morales found his workman among them.

"Say it!" he whispered to him.

"I saw them!" said the man, Jose. "I saw three Jews come out of here last night. I recognized one of them, named Ramon Levi. They were moving very quickly."

Shouts of vengeance filled the air as people moved toward the door. On the street, a mob of a hundred men formed and began running toward the Jewish district. They were joined by others along the way who carried clubs, axes, bricks, knives, swords. By the time they approached Marco's blacksmith shop the mob had become a screaming horde. "Kill the Jews! Enemies of God! Kill the filthy Jews!"

Ramon and his son Marco, in panic, blocked the entrance door and climbed a ladder that led to the roof. A group of men smashed the door, got to the roof and lunged for them. Father and son fought as well as they could but were overwhelmed and thrown to the crowd below. In a matter of seconds they were kicked, beaten, stabbed, rendered into unrecognizable bloody pulp.

Houses in the Juderia were burned, animals slaughtered. A throng entered the synagogue and smashed everything in sight. They wrote "Christ Killers" on the wall with blood from a praying man whose throat they had cut.

Daniel and Georgi saw it would be useless to try to escape as the mob swarmed toward their houses. Hastily, they led Anna, Wanda and Sofi into a storage cellar and locked it. Eli and Aron refused to get in with them.

"No. We're going to stay with you and fight," Aron said. Daniel looked at them with grief.

"All right, then."

They swung at their attackers bravely but futilly with

picks, hoes, and shovels, and were soon lying on the ground in pools of blood. Daniel had a knife in his back, Georgi's abdomen had been slashed, Eli's left arm had been virtually severed and his cheek and nose were smashed. Aron was bleeding from a hatchet wound to his forehead

The carnage went on until the attackers were satisfied and they went home to their Sunday dinners.

Aron stirred painfully, felt a lumpishness against his shoulder and realized Eli was lying alongside him.

"Are you dead?"

Eli didn't answer. Aron saw that Daniel and Georgi had been killed. He wished he was dead, too. Eli emitted a moan. Slowly, his head throbbing in pain, Aron wrapped his belt around Eli's mangled arm to stem its bleeding. Dizziness overcame him and he spiraled into utter darkness, wondering if it was death.

Morales' workman Jose was having bad dreams. He dreamed of rivers of blood cascading toward him, coming to drown him. He dreamed of flaming bodies coming out of burning houses. He dreamed he was pursued by mutilated corpses screaming in agony.

He awoke sweating after such dreams, afraid to go back to sleep. He reached for his wife for comfort but there was no comfort. When she asked, "what is it?" he said "nothing," turned aside, and stared fearfully into darkness.

During the day, he trembled and found it hard to think or talk to his family or other workmen at Morales' warehouse. He tried wine for relief but it brought no relief, it brought only vomiting and stumbling.

The voice was the worst part, the voice that asked, "What did you do?" Was it God? Did God hate him?

Morales approached him midday, before siesta, and observed him worriedly.

"What's wrong with you, Jose? You look terrible. Come into my office. Tell me what's wrong."

"It was a sin," said Jose. "God is angry."

"It was no sin," said Morales. "Jews are God's enemies. Look how they killed his son."

Jose turned his face away and said nothing. Morales took coins from a box.

"Look, you're nervous and exhausted. Here, take these and go on a holiday. Take all week. After resting, you'll feel better."

Jose took the money with trembling hands.

"Remember," said Morales, "you must never say anything to anybody about our secret because if you do you will lose your job and something even worse could happen to you and your family."

Jose gave the money to a beggar woman who stared at it in disbelief. He entered the cathedral and went into the bishop's office.

"I lied Father, it wasn't the Jews. Morales put chicken blood on the wafers and I said it was the Jews. God is angry."

"What? What are you saying? Are you losing your mind?"

"I think I am, but it's true. It wasn't the Jews, it was us."

The bishop studied Jose's anxious, emaciated face. He didn't want to believe the man's confession but he did.

"Why did you do it?"

"Morales wanted vengeance. He told me to help him."

The bishop paced, fingered his rosary, sat, paced again, stared out the window.

"Go now and keep your lips sealed. Say Hail Mary's repeatedly, for penance. This is between you and me and no one else. I will deal with Morales."

Jose walked to his house and sat against the wall, in the shade. He closed his eyes to test if he could sleep. The voice spoke to him again and he trembled and wept.

When it was dark he walked to Ramon's ravaged shop with a length of rope. He said "Forgive me," and hanged himself from a ceiling beam.

Jacobo gave Eli enough of Daniel's vodka to render him senseless and amputated the gangrenous arm below the shoulder, sealed the stump and bandaged it. Eli had screamed in pain even from a haze of alcohol, and fainted. Jacobo decided not to try to set the broken nose; Eli was breathing all right, and it wasn't too disfiguring.

"Will he live?" asked Anna. Her face was grey, her eyes sunken and bleary.

"Let's hope so. He's lost a lot of blood. He'll need to have meat and milk in the days to come."

"And where will we possibly get that?" she asked.

"I'll steal it," said Aron. The scar that went from his forehead to his scalp was raw and livid. The swelling around it had spread to an eyelid, giving him a look of menace.

Jacobo's assistant entered the room carrying a bundle wrapped in cloth. They knew it was Eli's excised arm. Jacobo told his assistant to take it to a field and bury it so that the animals couldn't get to it. Packs of rats and dogs drawn by bloodshed had been gnawing on corpses.

Jacobo, Sara and Pedro had returned a day after the mayhem, to the shocking sight of ruined buildings, plunder and death. Daniel's house was still standing, in shambles. The bodies of him and Georgi were lying on the floor covered with blankets, with candles burning alongside them. Anna, Wanda and Aron were sitting listlessly against a wall.

Sofi sat in a corner, hugging her father's jacket.

Pedro croaked, "Grandpa," shuddering and crying. Sara reached for him, her mind reeled, and she collapsed next to Daniel's body.

Aron, his voice detached and hollow, described what had happened. "Why?" asked Jacobo.

"We don't know," said Wanda.

At the end of their vigil, Jacobo said, "Let us remember how much we loved Daniel and Georgi. It will give us strength to carry on."

The flickering candles projected a dance of trembling shadows on the wall as the mourners drifted into fragments of sleep and woke to bottomless grief.

A few survivors took turns as sentries, keeping watch to alert neighbors if another attack should come. None did.

The truth about the wafers circulated after a Christian friend told Don Carlos Levi, a community leader, how it had happened that the Sunday worshippers exploded into a violent mob. He assured Don Carlos the danger was over.

The bishop had denounced the supposed desecration of the host as a "pious fraud" after learning Morales had tampered with it and forced his workman to lie. At the bishop's command, Morales signed a confession addressed to the citizens of the City of Verola. It was either that, the bishop had warned, or excommunication from the church, meaning eternal damnation and the torments of hell. After signing, Morales was turned over to the civil authorities, from whom he escaped, and fled to the north, with the help of a sympathetic prosecutor. In ten days, the husband of a murdered woman would track Morales down and kill him.

Jacobo, a neighboring doctor, and two assistants, worked to exhaustion tending to the wounded and seeing to it the dead were buried.

True to his word, Aron slipped into the homes of wealthy people when he knew they were gone, and stole bread, cuts of meat, jugs of milk. He stole some fine silk from Morales' warehouse, torched the building, and watched it burn to the ground from a distance, barely suppressing a shout of triumph.

The stolen nourishment had the hoped-for effect on Eli's health. His complexion was restored from grey to normal and brightness returned to his eyes. The stump of his arm was raw, slow in healing, but fortunately free of infection.

Daily, a contingent of Christians brought provisions and helped to clear debris and repair damaged buildings. Their help was donated and accepted with few words, as if to acknowledge that language was useless to assuage the horror that had transpired.

Aaron was making forays of theft every night except on Fridays. He held back on sabbath evenings, deciding not to tempt the evil eye. Not that he feared it—but then, who knows? He found that burglary came easily, almost naturally, to him, a matter of assessing risk and slipping in to take what was valuable. His range had expanded to include jewelry, precious metals and coins.. He felt no guilt, convinced it was more honorable to pilfer than do nothing at all.

Late one night in an alley near the Gothic Wall, he was aware of someone following him. The sound of footsteps stopped when he stopped and resumed when he resumed walking. He ducked into a doorway and waited. The footsteps got faster and closer. His pursuer turned a corner and looked about in confusion.

Aron exhaled a breath of relief. He wanted to laugh. "Pedro!"

Pedro scanned the darkness and saw Aron in the doorway. He smiled, walked over and poked Aron's shoulder.

"What are you doing here, Pedro?"

"I want to come with you. I want to steal things, too."

"How did you know I was doing this?"

"Everybody knows. Everybody knows you stole food,

and I saw you hide the other things in the cellar, and I saw you get them and sell them to the Greek."

"You're only eight years old, Pedro, you're too young."

"No I'm not. I can do it just like you, if you show me. I want to do it for grandpa and Georgi.

Aron debated with himself.

"All right, you can help me but you have to do exactly as I say, and you can't tell anyone. Agreed?"

"Agreed."

"Then listen, Pedro, the worst thing is dogs. When you see or hear dogs in a building, get out right away, because they can hurt you badly and their owners will catch you. The secret to stealing is to be quick and quiet. Always quick and quiet."

"Quick and quiet, Aron. I understand."

They walked softly down another street where a sign over a doorway said, Guerrero and Son, Religious Artifacts.

"This is the place," whispered Aron.

They stood in shadow listening and watching. It was that moment before entering a building when Aron would feel cold sweat on his back, followed by a lucid calmness. He knocked on the door and they waited. No answer, no dogs. He knocked again.

"Nobody in there," he whispered.

He pried the door with a metal bar and it sprang open. On a workbench were some cutting and engraving tools and an array of gold and silver crucifixes. Below was a box containing a bar of gold, a bar of silver, and some scrap. Aron placed the crucifixes in a sack, gave it to Pedro and picked up the box.

"Let's go," he said.

They moved quickly through the streets, merging with shadows until they arrived at their house.

"Give me the sack," said Aron. Pedro peered into it.

"Let me keep one. Just for tonight." Aron took out a cross.

"Just for tonight."

Pedro awoke in the morning with a sharp pain in his side. It was the crucifix, wedged between the mattress and his rib cage. He raised it to the light and admired how the golden body of Jesus gleamed on the silver cross.

Sara heard them slip into the house the following night. She got out of bed and went to the cellar.

"Mama!" Pedro exclaimed in surprise. He had been passing a roll of cloth to Aron. "You've been stealing with Aron!" said Sara.

"And you!" She slapped Aron. "You've been letting him help you! He could have been killed or imprisoned. Are you crazy or stupid, or both?"

Aron controlled his temper. "I know what I'm doing. I'm good at it and I look out for Pedro. When it's dangerous, I do it alone."

"No more! No more stealing, either of you. This is the end of it."

"Pedro, Do you understand me? No more stealing ever again. Do you understand me?"

"Yes I understand you. No more."

The rest of the household was roused by the commotion. They gathered in the cellar, sleepily.

"You all know I've been stealing from those murderers," Aron said. "Well look here.

Look what we have."

He lifted a board covering a hole in the floor and pulled up a metal box that was half-filled with coins.

"This is what the Greek paid for what I sold him. There's enough to keep us for years. We can go somewhere else and start over, and someday I can buy a ship, and earn my living at sea."

"Let's talk about this," said Jacobo. "Do we want to go somewhere else?"

"Yes!" exclaimed Sofi. No one argued.

"But where?" Jacobo asked.

"Do you know where I'd like to go?" asked Wanda. "To Granada. To the land of the Moors."

"Why there?" asked Anna.

"Because I just learned something. I'm pregnant." Oddly, she blushed.

"Praise the Lord," said Jacobo. "But what does that have to do with Granada?"

"It's far from here and a very different place. I don't want Daniel's baby born on the soil where he was killed."

"Well," Jacobo looked around him. "What about it?"

Eli moved to the center and squatted. The shirt sleeve where his arm would have been, swung emptily.

"Granada is a fine idea. I've heard the Muslims and Jews

live in harmony there and the land is graceful and fertile. It's synagogues are respected centers of learning and I could become a rabbi, some day."

Aron looked at him incredulously. "A rabbi? You still believe? You still think there's some God out there that gives a damn about us or anybody else?"

"Yes. I can't tell you why, but I do."

"Good luck with that," said Aron.

Eli turned to his mother. "What do you think? Would you like to go to Granada?"

"What can we lose?" said Anna. "It would be better than this graveyard."

"Much of the money I got from King Enrique went for medical supplies for victims of the attack but there's a considerable amount left," said Jacobo. "Enough to pay for a new beginning in life."

"More than enough," said Aron. "Combined with what I stole, we're wealthy."

"Then, let's stay together and go to Granada," said Sara, "or one day the police will come and drag off our pirates with their chest of gold."

They laughed, surprised to hear themselves laughing again.

The Jews of Granada spoke Arabic as well as a local variety of Spanish and the band from Verola found it difficult to converse with anyone in the bazaar until Isaac, a seller of cloth, overheard their stilted inquiries.

"I also came from Catalonia," he said, "and I heard you asking where you might go to rent a house. This is a fortunate encounter. I have a home that may be suitable for you."

The single-level house, set back from the Darro river between two hills, was built of adobe bricks, had a tile roof, and was arranged in a geometric design emulating the royal palace.

An Abyssinian cat sprang onto an open window and observed the strangers carefully.

"In Verola I fell in love with a Moorish woman, which eventually had troublesome consequences," Isaac said. "And so we came to Granada and married in her faith."

"It seems Jews are always getting into difficulties somewhere and then moving somewhere else," said Jacobo.

Isaac emitted a short laugh.

"True. But here there is acceptance and not many difficulties, as long as you respect the customs of Islam. Certainly, don't leer at women or insult Allah or his prophet, or be seen eating during a fast."

Isaac pointed toward a hill.

"That's the Albaicin district. The synagogue is just down the street from that large mosque. The present rabbinical staff has among its members a philosopher of great renown, though I can't think of his name at this moment. I fear I am not inclined toward scholarship. On the opposite hill is the Alhambra, the palace of King Boabdil. Jews are allowed to walk in the gardens but you may not enter any building unless invited."

"This house," he went on, "is spacious enough for you

to live in comfortably. Rent it if you like, and if you decide you want to buy it, we could work out the details. My wife died years ago and my daughter lives with her family in Almeria. I have taken a second wife, a widow, and we live in her smaller home."

"I wonder if there is room for another physician in this city," said Jacobo.

"We've had no plagues for many years, God be praised," said Isaac, "but people get sick and die, just like everywhere else. I'm sure your skills will be useful here."

Aron circled the house restlessly, went outside, swung from a tree branch, tired of that, and walked to the bank of the river. He squatted, plunked some stones into the water and decided the course of his life. He would stay with his family until they were well settled. In about six months, after Wanda gave birth to his half brother or sister, he would make his way to Malaga and apprentice himself as a sailor. When he was skilled at navigating a ship he would buy a vessel of his own.

Anna noticed Sofi standing in the doorway with the same abstracted expression Georgi often had, and the sadness returned, the sense of him gone forever. She thought he would have liked this graceful, tolerant place.

Wanda's pregnancy brought moments of dizziness early in the morning, but none of the nausea Sara used to complain of. She was certain she was forming a male child who would be the image of Daniel, broad and powerful, a man like an oak. It comforted her that she would never be alone now, even if she parted from the others.

Pedro walked down to the river, hearing Sara in the distance admonish him to be careful. A couple of boys watched him curiously and went back to their play. They were making boats from strips of bark, using leaves for sails and launching them on doomed voyages. The current overturned them, snagged them on branches, carried some downstream, out of sight. Pedro took off his clothes and waded up to his waist. He lost his balance on slippery stones and fell headlong into the river. The rapid flow thwarted his efforts to swim and carried him off as easily as a twig, knocking him into a pair of boulders, where he stopped. Gasping for breath, his nose bleeding, he struggled to the shore and lay there, contemplating the sky, astonished at its vibrancy, the intense blueness of it.

Ten years later Pedro fled Granada with a price on his head: One hundred gold dinars for the man who brought him back dead or alive to the wrathful father of exquisite Khadija.

A servant had spied Pedro and Khadija reveling in a passionate embrace. The servant, highly excited by the fervent display, watched through the slightly open door until his own arousal was unbearable and he masturbated. Thus relieved, he sped to inform his master of the scandalous liaison taking place in the bed chamber.

With marvelous timing, the lovers' ecstasy peaked deliriously just before they heard the din of father and servant yelling and running toward the site of their tryst. Pedro kissed the girl's forehead, grabbed his trousers, and was out the window and running when the door flew open. Khadija pulled the cover over her head and cried, "No! No!" as her father denounced her furiously and pounded on the wall.

"A harlot, a common whore, my own daughter! You take after your mother, the worst sort of mongrel bitch. I'll have that young man's head, I'll have his balls torn off, I'll see him roast in Hell!"

Pedro ran on the moonlit road away from Granada, toward the Sierra Nevada. He ran until he dropped in exhaustion, panting, holding the painful stitches in his side.

"Life is wonderful," he said, and the thought made him laugh.

He rolled over and bellowed loudly until a bush rustled with the flight of a scared fox.

He beheld the high mountains silhouetted ominously overhead in the night, and he laughed until he wept.

Sara invited Ahmed to sit, be comfortable, and not hesitate to eat his fill. He nodded and wolfed the food down ravenously, glancing at Sara and Jacobo occasionally as if to apologize for his appetite. When he finished he wiped his mouth with a bandana, leaned back in his chair and sighed.

"That was wonderful. I was very hungry."

"When you're ready, tell us how Pedro looks," said Jacobo. "Is he well?"

"Very well. He was thin when he came to us, but now he's as sturdy as you remember him. I think he's the largest man

I've ever seen in our region, and certainly the strongest. He's grown a beard; in that sense he has changed. He looks like one of the prophets of your Torah. But here, I should have given this to you right away."

He removed a letter from a leather pouch and handed it to Sara. She ran her fingers over it tenderly and passed it to Jacobo to read aloud.

"Greetings, dear family and friends. I greet you in the name of Allah, Jehovah, Lord Jesus, and all the creatures of land, sea and air. A strange way to begin a letter, I agree. I've been swayed by the rhapsodic verse of friend Ahmed the poet-messenger who delivered these words to you and may be with you as you read them."

Jacobo paused and nodded toward Ahmed.

"I know my absence of the last three months has been worrisome for you and I know I should have sent news before this, but one gets involved and time goes by.

"After my sublime but disastrous episode at the house of Khadija, I had no choice but to flee Granada. Certainly the wrath of her father was justified as was his desire to protect the virtue of his daughter, and certainly I'm a culprit deserving of exile. I miss you all very much and I'm sad I may never again set eyes on the kingdom of Granada, unless of course, Khadija's father should die, and the bounty on my head be lifted. "Think of it this way, dear parents, I'm worth a trove of gold and therefore not a complete failure.

"The night I left Granada I slept in a dry creek bed near a ravine where the wind whistled forlornly throughout the night. Several times, I woke to the sight of shiny animal eyes staring at me and I cried out in fear. Each time, the animals turned and ran, and I realized they were as afraid of me as I was of them. I made a blanket of pine branches to stop my shivering and slept peacefully until dawn. In the morning, I learned from piles of droppings that a variety of creatures had visited the creek bed to have a look at the baffling intruder.

"Since then, I've wondered what it meant to them to sniff and gaze upon the mysterious embodiment dumped in their midst. What, if anything, did they think?"

"I'm not used to hunger, and my first experience of it was difficult. For two days, I could find nothing to eat but mushrooms and berries that made me vomit and sweat.

The third day I caught a fat lizard, roasted it oever a small fire I built (after much struggle) and enjoyed it as much as the cuisine at King Enrique's palace. I've become a regular connoisseur of lizards. Also, I discovered that the roots that wild pigs scratch out of the ground are quite nourishing, though not very tasty. It's interesting how soon you learn to make do when you have to.

"I wandered east for five days, following the cleavage between two high mountains, shifting in mood from light-heartedness to despondency. There is a wonder and a terror in being cut loose from the comforts and habits of a lifetime. One morning, I sighted an ibex watching me climb and my heart leapt in joy. It was like finding a lost friend. I ran toward it calling, 'Ram! Ram! Wait, I'm coming!' It watched me for a few moments, ran off, and I conceded it was an animal and I was a man, and that was that.

"My first meeting with a human came near the end of a

week at a cave overlooking a narrow valley. Somehow, when I saw the cave I was sure someone would be in it. He had long grey hair, a grey beard, was tall and lean, had a scarred cheek. His eyes were golden brown and seemed to gaze beyond the present into some other realm. He wore a sort of robe made from deerskin and spoke in fragmented sentences, often just a word or two. When I came upon him he was sitting cross-legged near the opening of the cave, grinding some roots into a powder. He gestured for me to sit.

"Who?" he asked.

"I explained myself as well as I could and recounted the events leading to the moment. He nodded and grunted as though it was an old story.

"'Two days,' he said, 'And then you go.'

"In the next two days I put together from bits and pieces that his name was Carmino, he had been a Dominican priest, defrocked for some unorthodox view, and banished from Castile. He enlisted as a soldier in Aragon, was wounded in battle and left to die. Determined to live, he and some other wounded men ate the raw flesh of a cavalryman's slain horse. He crawled about on the battlefield and searched dead soldiers for money until he had an impressive sum. He made his way to Valencia, boarded a Venetian ship to Malaga, and traveled to Granada where he learned Arabic, invested in a vineyard, converted to Islam and married. His wife, only nineteen years old, died in childbirth. Despondent, he gave the child over to the care of his in-laws and set out for the mountains. That was twenty years ago.

"Despite his grey hair, he has a youthful, smooth

countenance, as though a young man were masquerading as old. My efforts to draw him into dialogue, gauge his thinking, his spiritual contentions, were fruitless, but he did pass on something valuable to me in an oblique way. It seems clear that in no longer striving or craving anything, he had reached a sort of freedom. I think of the Christian scripture, "Blessed are the pure in heart, for they shall know God."

"When we parted he touched my head and looked directly into my eyes for the first time. I had a wondrous moment of vastness, of expansion far beyond the boundaries of myself.

"I climbed downward the rest of the day toward a narrow valley and made my roost near a stream where a doe and her fawn were having a drink. Instead of running from me, they stayed in place, drinking peacefully. The doe allowed me to come forward and visit until she decided it was enough, and stamped a hoof.

"Observing the stars that evening and listening to the rhythmic current of the stream, the world seemed like some magical spell cast by Carmino.

"Please be sure to pass this letter on to Eli, our esteemed rabbi of imponderables. "Eli, the visions of the prophets, their divine madness, seem plausible in this wilderness. Ordinary logic retreats and a different way of understanding seeps through. The Torah you tutored me in so patiently seems but a pale reflection of the awesome power of creation, forever changing, ever beyond our small concerns. Lest I sound like a wise fool of philosophy, let me surmise that your study of kabbalah and meditation on the Absolute have surely brought your mind to a place beyond my meager comprehension. I hope you're not disappointed by my misadventures, rabbi, and my fall from grace as your student protegee. After all, one does not love God less if he loves a woman. But then, if one transgresses, he must pay the price, and here I am, a stranger in a strange land, (Moses, Book 2, you see, I did learn something) a nobody, dust in a cosmic sandstorm.

"I'll tell you, family and friends, what I am. I'm a goatherd. Every day, I keep watch over a hundred goats as they forage on nearby meadows and hills. I'm coming to know as much about goats as I do about people. When one of the herd is killed by a lion or wolf, I grieve just as its relatives, though I myself slaughter goats, eat their meat, drink their milk, wear their skins. What terrible business, all this killing and eating.

"These goats belong to Muzaffar, the father of Ahmed. He has permitted Ahmed to go to Granada and enlist as a soldier. There are still three sons to work the land and oversee the flocks. Ahmed is restless, I think, and has a yen for glory. He believes Granada is in grave danger from Castile, as I'm sure he will explain to you.

"I came upon this family after wandering for ten days. At the end of the canyon I described was a wall of rock with an opening barely enough for a man to squeeze through. On the other side—I could barely believe my eyes—was a scene of idyllic beauty, a farm, a pond, a corral, a magnificent house of stone. I entreated Muzaffar, master of the land, that I might perform labor for some food, and here I am yet, working and eating.

"Muzaffar is a Sufi contemplative, and is patiently

attempting to instruct me in ruyat alqub, the vision of the heart. This practice, he says, will make one more open to the presence of God, but to be honest, my heart has been opened by Zorayda, his youngest daughter. She has almond eyes, hair of spun black silk, a gentle smile, and a semblance like sparkling dew. However, she's promised to one Mahmoud, and fate has decreed that I shall not marry into this excellent family.

"And so, my beloved relatives and friends, I wish you well. I miss you. I will be leaving here soon, as I could not bear to attend Zorayda's wedding. There is much I have to learn and do in this world, and I will be traveling for some time. I hope to get to Egypt and the Holy Land and the fabled islands of Homer. My first goal is to reach Malaga and link up with Aron. I'll sail with him to whatever port he's headed for.

"Farewell for now. May God keep you. Pedro"

Aron was hunched over a table in his ship's cabin, calculating figures and making entries in a ledger. He sipped from a bottle of grappa intermittently, and breathed a sigh of satisfaction. A large shadow suddenly cast on the wall, startled him, and he swiveled around.

"Hello uncle!"

"Pedro!"

Aron sprang up so quickly the grappa bottle rocked and nearly toppled. "I'll be damned!"

They embraced with laughs and back slaps, swaying with the roll of the ship. "Here, sit. Have a drink of this. How did you find me?"

"It was easy. I asked some captains where the Star of Esther was berthed. One old sailor said, 'That'd be the ship of Scarface' and pointed me in the right direction."

Aron traced the scar on his forehead.

"Scarface. Is that what they call me? I guess they could call me worse. What are you doing in Malaga?"

"I came to find you and sail with you, wherever you're going. Where are you going next?"

"Sardinia, with a load of leather and furs."

"That's perfect. It'll point me toward Egypt and the Levant."

"Wait a minute. Slow down. Why do you want to go there? In fact, why do you want to go anywhere?"

Pedro sighed, took a sip of grappa and unraveled the story. The ship's mascot, a gray-striped cat, jumped onto his lap and dozed, indifferent to history.

"And so I rode into Malaga this morning on the mule that Muzaffar gave me and sold it for a good price. I've got some money, I've got health, I've got time and a whole world."

"Pedro, do you remember how furious Sara got when she found out you went stealing with me? How do you think she'll take it, me dropping you off in the middle of nowhere?"

"It's not nowhere, it's somewhere. Don't worry, it's good for her as well as for me. There are people with swords around here who would gladly trade my head for a fat reward."

"All right, you're aboard. I'll pay you sailor's wages to Sardinia. I run a tight ship. If any of the other sailors gives you any trouble, we'll throw him overboard."

The house in Granada looked just as it had when Aron had last seen it nine years before. The furniture was in the same place, the same plants dangled from baskets, the copper pots and kettles gleamed still from their hooks over the hearth and the lemon tree that shaded and scented a space by the front door was implacably the same.

Aron was struck by the difference between the sameness of the scene, and the people who lived in it. Everyone was changed considerably, most obviously Wanda's son Adam, his half brother. He had last seen the boy as a toddler and now he was ten years old, a sturdy fellow resembling Daniel. Of the women, Anna had aged most noticeably. Her hair had gone grey and her eyes were shadowed from a habit of melancholy. In contrast, Wanda appeared hale, though she had put on weight, and her copper hair was intermingled with streaks of silver. Sofi, seated beside her husband Marcus, a builder, had grown into a fine-looking woman with Slavic features resembling those of Georgi. Her usual loquacity was subdued, perhaps in deference to Marcus, a witty fellow who liked to talk. She held a five-month-old baby girl in her arms. Eli, as yet unmarried, had grown an elegant curly beard that counterbalanced the increasing baldness on his skull. Aron saw that he still had a dreamy, ascetic expression on his face. Jacobo's carrot-colored hair was tinged with frost at the temples and he had developed a respectable belly. The change in Sara was more subtle than in the others. Not yet grey or heavy or lined, she had been transformed by a burden of sorrow. An aura of sadness emanated from her almost as a halo. Aron noticed she sometimes slipped into an abstracted silence and brought herself back to the present with an effort.

Aron pushed his plate away, downed the remaining nectar, leaned forward on his elbows and scanned the eyes of his companions.

"After we docked at Sardinia, Pedro helped us unload our cargo and take on fresh food and water. He slept aboard two more nights, until I sailed toward Naples. I had introduced him to the captain of a larger ship, who signed him on for a voyage to Alexandria.

"Fourteen months after that, I sailed into Alexandria myself and went looking for him.

I didn't have much luck until I was sitting in a tavern one day, and asked the owner, a one-eyed Algerian, if he'd seen anybody matching Pedro's description. He burst out laughing and poured me another drink, free. He said, 'Pedro, yes I know him. He came in here all the time. He was tall and wide as a door, he had a thick black beard, and he made crazy jokes, like the time he said the bar was too long and he sawed away two inches of it.'

"The Algerian told me there was this Academy of Knowledge where Pedro hung out with a bunch of scholars when he wasn't carousing around. I found the place. It was run by a Coptic Christian, a Muslim mullah, and a rabbi. A plaque on the wall said, 'Dedicated to the Betterment of all Mankind.' A flowered courtyard, where some men were reading and talking, led to a huge library room, surrounded by books and scrolls.

The rabbi was at a table writing something, so lost in it that I had to tap his back to get his attention. I told him I was Pedro's uncle and was trying to find him. The rabbi sighed and said, 'Pedro, yes, he was one of our promising students, but he's gone now, he's gone to Gizeh.'

"Gizeh, that's where these huge pyramids are, the ancient tombs of pharaohs. It's in the desert but near the Nile river and the city of Cairo. By this time I was determined to find Pedro, and I thought, what the devil, I've never seen a hippo or a crocodile or a vast desert, all I ever see is seas and seaports, so I put my ship on drydock and set off with two camels and a guide and went to Gizeh. The only words I could understand from the guide, Abdul, were, 'We go that way. Now we eat. Now we sleep.'

"As it turned out, my timing was lucky. A few more days and Pedro would have been gone, off to the Holy Land. He had been living with a monastic cult that worshiped the sun and moon and he was fed up. This was a weird ragbag of people, if you ask me, a mixture of Egyptians, Jews, one Greek, and two Armenians. One of the Armenians, a skinny guy named Aram, was the leader of the cult. He had some strange power to sway people. He claimed God dwelled in the sun by day and the moon by night, and would transform humans into immortals if they worshipped His rays. The group lived in brick huts arranged in a semicircle and they contemplated the sunrise every morning with a cloth over their eyes, so as not to go blind. They did the same when the sun went down in the evening, and every night they would gaze at the moon until it disappeared behind the pyramid of Cheops. Adam claimed that when the moon was in its lesser phases, God was extending Himself to other parts of the universe, but never abandoned his true worshippers.

To tell you the truth, I thought Aram was a complete lunatic. He was intelligent, I admit, and friendly, but he was also insane. People from the river area came up every day with food and water, and treated him like he was a king. They bowed, and he bestowed blessings on him, and I was flabbergasted by it.

"Pedro saw the light ten days before I came, when he was bitten by a serpent. The poison put him in a delirium and fever, but it also cleared his mind and put things in perspective. He told me, 'I had visions of a grand delusion, all of us trying to get a prize that's not allowed to the rest of humanity, and I saw Aram as the most pathetic of all. I saw he would fall apart if his system of belief crumbled away. The saddest revelation was that Aram's role as a priest was a weakness. He simply wasn't strong enough to live as a man with it's ambiguity and loneliness.'

"I gave Pedro some silver money and a lucky charm I'd picked up in Algiers, and he joined a caravan headed for Jerusalem with perfume and silk. They traveled at night to avoid the searing heat. The sky was black like velvet the night they left, and the stars were diamond bright. When the caravan was out of sight I could still smell the perfume. In fact, I smelled it all the way back to Alexandria."

Aron faced Sara.

"He said to tell you nothing could harm him. He said when he finds what he's looking for, he'll return to Spain and you'll see him. I believe it. He'll be back."

Sara got up from the table and went outside to the lemon tree. She picked a ripe one as high as she could reach, and walked down to the river. She felt herself lighten, as though she could float in the air. She peeled the lemon, made a neat mound of the rinds, and ate the sections slowly. She wondered why lemon juice was welling up in her eyes and trickling down her cheeks.

Amos' tough-looking swarthy face belied the gentle visionary within. The man who was renowned as a learned mystic looked as though he could be a bandit in the wilds of Judea. He and his student stood at a tower on the Wall of Jerusalem and gazed toward Mount Moriah.

"I don't accept the story of Abraham and Isaac the way it's written," Amos said. "Anybody can obey God. It doesn't prove anything. I pondered it for years and I came to the unshakable conviction that Abraham defied God, and God was pleased."

"You can see it in your mind's eye. In the blackest night, when all hope is drained from the universe, Abraham unties his son, embraces him, and sends him down the mountain,

"'Go,' he says. 'Go back to your mother.'

"When the boy is gone, Abraham shouts into the abyss, 'If you want a sacrifice, take me. I will not give you my son.'

"At wit's end, he plunges the knife into his own chest, and the knife falls out. There is no blood, no pain, no scar. Instead, the blade has severed his fear, his anger, his pride, and there is nothing left but compassion for all creation. In the years to come, Abraham tries to communicate this oneness but he's misunderstood. He doesn't teach that there is one God, he teaches that God is One, and people aren't ready to comprehend it."

The night was hauntingly black and Mount Moriah hovered forlornly. Pedro, suddenly depressed, stood at the base, pondering what to do. His body didn't want to move, his resolve had dissolved into torpor. With a near-heroic effort, he leaned forward and began walking. Slowly, he trudged upward, feeling as though a force was pushing against him. Halfway up the mountain, sweating, he took off his caftan, draped it over his shoulder, and proceeded upward, wearing just a loincloth.

At the top, the landscape around Jerusalem looked amorphous like the obscure unknowable forms of a dream. A shepherd's fire flickered to the east, sparks of hope in the middle of nowhere. A chill in the air brought goosebumps to Pedro's flesh, and he put on his caftan. He found a ledge below the crest that was sheltered from the wind and sat there cross legged, staring into the night. The depression had lifted during the climb and now he felt nothing, as though a plug had been pulled, and his feelings drained.

"Where is the God of Abraham?"

The sound of his voice jarred the night and the God of Abraham answered with silence. Pedro realized he must be silent, too.

His thoughts and impressions slid past mundane boundaries, pouring forth without logic, a stream of phantasmagoria in vivid colors, childhood scenes dissolving into swirling clouds, naked dancers rising out of graveyards, ponderous voices exhorting nonsense, journeys without goal, places without name. Finally, a vision of thunder and lightning, rain cascading, cleansing all, and the brilliant gold of the sun banishing shadows, revealing crystalline, absolute being.

Profound silence beyond conception.

He dwelled in that state throughout the night, barely moving. With the light of dawn, he rose, stretched, and contemplated the world around him. On the plain below, on the mountain, in himself, there was no separation, there was no condition other than God.

He walked down the mountain feeling as light as air, and pondered how he could help people to understand.

Fray Tomas de Torquemada told the servant to keep piling more wood on the fire until it became a blazing conflagration. The servant feared it would char the elegant tile fireplace but did as he was told, adding sticks and logs until it raged like the fire of Hell, its reflection gleaming diabolically in the eyes of priest and servant.

"Go now," said the priest.

Torquemada gazed at the fire in fascination for perhaps an hour, occasionally interrupting the sound of burning, crackling wood with a cough. Some of the sparks leaped from the fireplace, flew halfway across the room and died on the tile floor, prompting a snort of amusement from the priest.

He read the papal brief again. As before, it proclaimed that Torquemada was appointed Grand Inquisitor of Spain as of October, 1483. It raised him from a local inquisitor to head of all the Inquisition in Castile, Leon, Aragon, Catalonia and Valencia. In effect, it was his show.

When Queen Isabella warned the clergy against excesses after the pope had formally permitted Spain to hold the Inquisition five years before, Torquemada had assured her there could be no excess of righteous zeal for the Holy Church and the purity of Spain.

"These heretics, my lady, they befoul this land with hypocrisy, they deal the Church two-faced contempt. The very existence of backsliding Jewish Marranos and Muslim Moriscos shames the Christian faith they claim to love. Their secret practices are hateful to the sanctity of our Lord."

"I'm not known as Isabella the Catholic because of the weakness of my faith," said the queen. "Nor am I naive. I know that many conversos are Christians in name only. I also know that priests are human and capable of acting out of spite. I want the Inquisition to be just, and conducted in lawful order."

"And so it shall be," said Torquemada.

After he left the throne room he wondered why

Fernando, the usually talkative king, had not spoken, and had seemed to regard him with distaste. He'd have to be politic with the royal couple, he realized. They weren't afraid of wielding power, as Enrique, Isabella's half-brother, had been. Abruptly, he stopped, and slapped his forehead.

"What a fool I am!" he shouted. A passing maid looked at him with alarm.

He remembered, with a shock, that King Fernando had Jewish blood in his veins, as did he himself, and that he Torquemada, had pronounced Jewish Marranos—the term meaning pigs, as well as converts—with icy contempt.

"But then," he muttered, "perhaps Fernando resents my long acquaintance with Isabella, and my influence on her."

Charmed by the red, yellow, orange and blue flames leaping from the burning wood, Torquemada settled into benign relaxation and considered progress: So far, hundreds of unrepentant heretics burned alive and it has just begun. In time, thousands more will be paraded to the stake. They call it a reign of terror but that's a poor understanding. Truly, it's a reign of mercy to burn away sin, to destroy evil, is it not? Everywhere, tribunals are carefully examining evidence, convicting heretics and staging *auto da fe* processions of penitents in humiliating *sambenito* garments flogging themselves, marching to the square where the unrepentant among them are submitted to the agony of fire. Even here, there is mercy, for we allow those who confess at the last moment to be strangled before burning, thereby sparing them pain. And those who confess to everything and name other secret Judiazers or Mohammedans, we give them justice fitting each case—fines, imprisonment, the galleys, scourging by whip, exile. And the torture? I have no regrets. Without it, few would confess. A man whose limbs are tearing apart will give up secrets gladly. Yes, they inform on their children, their parents, their lovers, their priests, their friends and neighbors. Those few who can prove their innocence are sent back to their lives, their confiscated property returned to them. What could be fairer than that?

The fire was burning quietly; it would soon go out. Whether to call the servant for more wood or let it expire? Torquemada closed his eyes and hummed a lullaby his mother used to sing to him. In a few minutes he was asleep.

It had not been Pedro's intention to start a cult. One thing had led to another and it had happened. Some enthusiastic followers had spread the notion he was the new Savior, known as El Amigo, and the idea caught on and circulated. Drawings of his face, looking absurdly saintly, he thought, turned up randomly throughout the land and brought hope to the hopeful and the cynical.

"El Amigo will bring the message of brotherhood to all the world and end the cruel Inquisition," people were saying.

At a time when no more than an accusation by a spiteful neighbor or debtor could land one in the dungeons and torture chambers of the Inquisition, fearful souls yearned for the intervention or a compassionate friend and God had sent them El Amigo. So was it said.

What was the message of this savior?

"We are joined in one divine field of creation where there is nothing but the Absolute.

When we cut through self-centeredness to the core of our being, we discover that the essence that moves the universe moves also in us.

"Religions can help us along the way but they can also prompt us to become contemptuous of others. It is no better to be a Christian than a Muslim or a Jew and no better to be a Jew or Muslim than a Christian. Treat others as you would like to be treated, that's the highest religion."

In the beginning, a few seekers drawn by Pedro's words and his charisma came to sit and talk with him in his wood-carving shop in Almeria. Gradually they brought friends, and the weekly gatherings burgeoned into an event known as the Abode of Light. Some devotees helped Pedro knock out a wall of his shop and extend the building so that an increasing crowd could fit in. Those who came were a mixed assortment of humanity. Students, laborers, poets, artists, prostitutes, petty thieves, mingled with members of bourgeois respectability and there were some who treaded a shadowy world between madness and sanity.

The meetings followed a similar pattern each week. Some of the talented would play music and sing, or recite poetry. After that, Pedro would ask his visitors to sit in silence for a while and watch their thoughts flit about. He commented that though thoughts and bodily discomforts might distract them, even those arose from the formative mystery of Creation. At a signal, his helper Yesenia concluded the silences with a soft clash of cymbals. After the subsequent murmuring and stretching subsided, Pedro gave a talk that may have seemed perplexing to some, and he addressed their questions.

"You ask what freedom is, and I ask you this: How can we be free when self-absorption builds a wall around us and confines us? This wall has a frame of aggression and defensiveness and its fabric is ignorance and distrust. You may remember the story of the man who went to borrow a hoe from his neighbor. As he walked, he fretted that the neighbor might refuse him, and he became very angry. When his neighbor came to the door, the man shouted, "I wouldn't take your filthy hoe if you gave it to me!"

"We're laughing at this deluded man and that's healthy and wise because we're also laughing at our own delusions and the traps they get us into. The more self-centered nonsense we let go of, the greater we become in spirit."

"How do you know these things?" a listener asked. "You speak like a prophet. Are you a prophet?"

"I'm an ordinary man like yourself but I've been very fortunate. I had an experience in Jerusalem that opened my eyes."

"Why do you have these meetings?" asked another. "Do you want to have power over others? Does it flatter you?"

"It's natural to want to share a vision that can help others. Power is not mine to have. Power simply is. We exist within power like fishes in the sea."

"What is sin?" was the final question.

"I call it sin when you don't treat others the way you

would like to be treated."

After the questions and a brief period of silence, they partook of bread and wine and filed out quietly, some struggling with inner demons, some confused, others exultant or peaceful.

A young student of the Koran aspiring to become a mullah, sardonically dubbed "Yussef the brilliant" by his peers, lingered behind and approached Pedro.

"Why do you simplify the vast realm of religious thought in such a way? You transpose the complexities of scripture and exegesis into terms attuned to a child's understanding."

"I understand your concern," said Pedro, "and I have nothing against scholarly disputation, but children understand with the heart. If adults can recover that, perhaps it will ease their suffering and help them to see in a fresh way."

Yussef the Brilliant pondered the response, shrugged, and walked off.

Yesenia, the lovely green-eyed servant of Don Francisco the glassmaker, stayed behind each week, tidied the hall and swept the floor. After cleaning, she locked the doors, closed the curtains and stood before Pedro so he could remove her dress.

When she was bare, he would stroke her body until their arousal was incandescent, and they would make love in joyful abandon.

"Well, if you're a saint, you're a goat saint," she murmured on the first night.

"I'm no saint, I'm a man. Who wants to be a saint, bloodless and pious, enshrined in a stained glass window?"

"The other women, I bet they'd like to sleep with you, too. I bet they dream about it."

"Shut up and kiss me, Yesenia, or I'll sulk. I'll get rough. I'll break your broom into pieces and throw them into the fire." She giggled and rolled on top of him.

"If those other women knew what I was doing here, they would be jealous, Pedro.

You don't know how jealous they would be."

"You're jealous of their jealousy."

"Yes!"

"Hah!"

"I love you."

"Then prove it. Let me in again."

"No. Not until you tell me how much you love me."

"I love you as much as a hundred canaries whistling at the stars on the first night of spring when there's a soft breeze and the fragrance of gardenias fills the air and the donkey is singing his heart out."

"You might be interested in what's happening in Almeria, Rabbi." The student put a drawing on the table.

"This man they call El Amigo, they claim he's the new savior. He's a woodcarver, a Spanish Jew who studied with sages in Egypt and Palestine. He teaches a kind of monism, that everything is an aspect of God. My cousin tells me he's a large man of about thirty with great humor and energy, very compelling, who generates a powerful message."

Eli stared at the picture in disbelief.

"That's Pedro! Pedro Stefanek, the son of Sara! You know his family yourself!"

Eli rose from his seat, walked to the door, kicked it shut, and came back for another look. Yes, it was him.

"Where did you get this?"

"I told you, from my cousin. He sent it from Almeria. He has met El Amigo and was very impressed with him."

"This is amazing, amazing!"

Eli took the picture and hurried to the street. He wound his way down the hill from the Albaicin district in such haste that people turned to stare,

He knocked loudly.

"Sara, Jacobo, open the door. It's me, Eli."

"Eli, what is it?"

Sara opened the door as one of Jacobo's patients hobbled out on crutches, his face drawn in pain.

"Keep your weight off your leg as much as you can, Haqim, and don't get into any more fights with mules."

"Yes doctor, assuredly. Thank you."

"Sit down and brace yourselves," Eli said. "I have a wonderful surprise."

"All right, we're seated and braced," said Jacobo. "What is it?"

"This!"

Eli brandished the drawing.

"My God!" gasped Sara. "Where did you get this?"

"A student showed it to me. Apparently pictures like this are finding their way around Spain. It seems Pedro has become a renowned teacher of the spirit."

"Where is he?"

"In Almeria. He earns his living as a woodcarver as did Daniel, may he rest in peace."

"Almeria, that can't be far. We must go there," said Sara. "We must go immediately."

"I agree. What do you think, Jacobo?"

"Much as I love Pedro, I think I must stay with my patients. Two of them are hovering near death. But you go, by all means, the two of you. It's the best thing to do, though I'll be lost without Sara."

"We'll leave tomorrow morning," said Sara. "Can you be ready?"

"Certainly," said Eli. "I'll turn everything over to my assistant."

Eli tucked the empty sleeve that dangled from his left shoulder into his sash, and smiled at Sara.

"He's called El Amigo by his followers. Soon El amigo will be joined by a one-armed rabbi and a blue-eyed mama."

Sara studied the picture closely. It was an accurate rendering, unmistakably Pedro, though she had never seen him before with a beard. She remembered the predictions of old Rabbi Lohman and the seer Maria. How did they know? Her eyes sparkled, a rosy hue glowed on her face. She realized she was truly happy for the first time in many years.

Eli was glad to get away from his synagogue duties of

scholarship, ceremony, and arbitrating an endless stream of social dilemmas. He found it pleasant to be a nobody again, living in the moment, free of responsibility. He strolled about Almeria, helped Pedro in his workshop and wrote verse as it came to him. He had satisfied himself that Pedro's enlightenment was genuine by his lack of arrogance, his obvious inner peace, and his indifference to what people thought of him. He saw that people instinctively trusted Pedro and seemed to thrive in his presence. Eli himself was imbued these days with a poignant sense of something spacious, fresh, essentially holy. It felt as basic as his breath and flowed through him beyond the rumblings of intellect and imagination.

Sara too had been lifted to a dimension where the ordinary had become sacred, exquisite. It exceeded the delight of being reunited with her son; it was an arrival from the usual constricted world to an open boundless one. People were a revelation to her now, the way they carried on, their variety, their energies. It was clear to her that all their psychic convolutions, their aspirations, even when wicked, were emanations from an ocean of Being, and they were unaware of it.

She and Eli had decided they would stay in Almeria for one month and return then to Granada, which was endangered by the likelihood of a siege from Castile. It was uncertain whether the Muslim kingdom could last the year. Already, troops of Fernando and Isabella had captured some southern towns and the port of Malaga, cutting off essential supplies. Sara wanted to be with Jacobo when and if the city fell so that they could decide together whether to remain or leave. Eli doubted the Crown would tolerate an

Arabic-Jewish culture on conquered land for more than a short while. There was speculation the royal couple was considering an edict to expel all unconverted Jews and Muslims from Spain, but that was as yet rumor, time would tell.

In the meantime, they basked in their time in Almeria, an enchanted interlude, as Eli put it.

"Pedro, what will happen to you?" Sara asked him one day. "Sooner or later the authorities will despise and distort what you say and the effect it has on people. It worries me."

"You don't have to worry, mama, but you're right. They're closing in. Recently, two clerics from the Holy Office have attended our meetings in disguise, to gather evidence against me."

"I know who you mean," said Eli. "They sit in the back, against the wall. I've noticed how one takes notes and the other scrutinizes the audience. I've dubbed them Stern and Sour."

"Yes, well they won't be back, they found what they were looking for."

"Then you must flee from here," said Sara.

"I can't. Yesterday some agents from Militia Christi seized Yesenia at her home and took her to Valencia to stand for questioning. They'll want to use her as an example—a Christian who supposedly compromised her faith under the sway of a mad, persuasive Jew.

Our final meeting will be tomorrow night, so that I can say farewell and urge our friends to follow their own vision, and then I'm going into hiding. Eli, I'd like you to bring the Holy Office the message that I'll give myself up if they release Yesenia with a certificate of innocence. I want her out before they torture her."

"But they'll torture you," said Sara.

"No, mama, they won't. Believe me, they have plenty of evidence for whatever case they want to make."

Eli noted that Pedro's transformation didn't prevent him from stretching the truth. "Pedro, listen to me," said Eli. "They don't want people to think for themselves. They want conformity to dogma. In their eyes you represent evil incarnate, Satan tempting the flock to stray. It's not only the Church. The rabbis and mullahs, too, will revile and disown you. If you let the Inquisition get hold of you, it'll crush you."

"It's going to turn out all right, I know it. It has to be this way; it's a quirk of history. Mama, stop weeping. Trust me."

"This is our last communion, our final meeting. Some foes of our quest for essential being have flushed out our nest, and they didn't like what they found. If we meet any longer, we'll be inviting persecution and martyrdom and we don't want that, it's useless. Our purpose has been to hallow our daily lives, not sacrifice them to terror. Whatever you've gained here you'll always have, and in subtle ways, it'll spark off you and help others.

"The world is ever new, eternally a wonder, yet mankind is fumbling in the dark and it will be ages before it finds its way to the light. For centuries to come, societies will continue to plague one another with despotism, warfare, intolerance, deceit, and every other conceivable madness.

"All this travail arises out of the mistaken notion that we are separate from one another and separate from eternity. You might wonder, 'If this is all but a play in eternity, how can we interfere?' and I submit there's a world of difference between saying that and knowing that. It's as different as being awake and being asleep.

"None of you has come here by accident though it may seem that you have. From the moment you were born, every single event of your lives has worked to form you a certain way and bring you to this place at this time. From this day forward, how you go on is up to you.

"My advice is always be aware that time is precious, and use it wisely. What good does it do to spend your time in a stupor of selfishness? Observe constantly how you think, feel, and behave, and see how your actions affect those around you.

"When you change, everyone else changes. It's remarkable, how a tiny candle has the power to illuminate darkness. And so, one compassionate person can enter a room and lighten the burden of others without saying a word.

"When your faith gets weak, when all conscious effort seems pointless and tiring, take refuge in the silence of your innermost self. The deeper you go, the vaster you become until there is only the understanding beyond words.

"Tonight, my friends, we'll take our bread and wine in silence and depart. It has been the joy of my life to spend time with you."

Guido the Illuminist squinted his eyes in pain when the door creaked open to allow Pedro into the dungeon. He had not seen such a flood of light for ten days, when he was last tortured. He was relieved to see the guard had not come to drag him away but to bring a new prisoner, and his heart stopped pounding so rapidly. In the sudden infusion of light, Pedro was both bright and indistinct, a large entity swaddled in curling rays of energy. Guido blinked, shook his head, and tried to focus on the new presence to determine if it was in fact an archangel.

"Here's some company, Guido, you Italian pig. This is El Amigo. You two sweethearts will like each other."

He beckoned to a short stocky prisoner with a brutally scarred face who was standing in the doorway.

"Okay, Miguel, carry out the shit."

Miguel lifted the bucket of excrement, urine and vomit from a hole in the floor and replaced it with an empty one. When he and the guard were out of the cell they slammed the door loudly and locked it.

"Phew! What a smell! Keep your distance, Miguel."

Their voices echoed off the corridor walls as they clacked down the narrow stairway.

In the accustomed dim light Guido saw that Pedro was in fact a man and not a supernatural apparition.

"Welcome to Purgatory," said Guido.

"Thank you. Kind of you to invite me."

A moment's silence, and they burst into laughter.

"Well, what infamy have they blamed on you?" asked Pedro.

"Heresy. I'm a standard case. In Rome I was a member of the Illuminati, who believe intense prayer and purification are the best avenues to Christ, rather than entrenched dogma and a show of piety. The powers that be were not happy with that and our members were harassed, arrested, and persecuted. I escaped to Aragon and one day I explained my convictions to an acquaintance who turned out to be an informer for the Holy Office."

"These are difficult times."

"The worst. And you? What is it they hate about you?"

Pedro summarized the events from the night he left Granada to the present. "And like you, I talked myself into trouble."

"So far," said Guido, "I've been given the water torture, where they put a cloth on your mouth and pour water on it until you nearly suffocate. And the rack, pulling my limbs, but stopping short of tearing them apart. If they start to apply the fire to my feet, I think I'll just confess and repent. I'm weak. There's a limit to what I can stand. Do you think I'm wrong?"

"No, I don't think there's any use for you to suffer more."

"What will you do if they torture you?"

"I don't know."

"Do you know something? Whether I'm weak or strong, Christ lives in this dungeon with me. Day and night, I feel him illuminating my being, sustaining the whole world, and I feel blessed. Do you know what I mean?"

"Yes, the primal spirit. I feel it always. What else is there?"

The faces of Fray Alonso and Fray Rodrigo revealed their fear when the Grand Inquisitor entered the room and nodded at them. Was that contempt in his eyes? Why had he come all the way from Segovia to take part in this tribunal?

Torquemada didn't try to put them at ease.

"When this Pedro Stefanek, the one they call El Amigo, is brought in, I'll do all the questioning. Is that clear?"

They allowed that it was clear. "Bring him in."

The door opened and Pedro was led in. He was pale, had lost considerable weight. His dark sunken eyes conveyed a mixture of suffering and humor. The guards placed him before the inquisitors at a long table and stepped back, against the wall.

The Grand Inquisitor pursed his lips and pressed a finger against them, studying Pedro with great interest.

"Why do they call you El Amigo?"

"Probably because I believe people should be friendly toward one another."

"Should you and I be friends?"

"Sure. Why not?"

Torquemada leaned back and laughed loudly. His abrupt uncharacteristic reaction broke the tension and the others laughed, too.

Just as suddenly, Torquemada stopped laughing and pounded the table.

"Quiet! This tribunal charges that you have committed blasphemy and that you have worked insidiously, and with sorcery, to undermine the faith of Christians. Do you deny it?"

"I deny it."

"Do you deny that you used your satanic powers to cast a spell on naive Christians at your so-called meetings of the spirit?"

"I deny that too. Your informers must have told you that Muslims and Jews were present, as well as Christians. Why would I cast a spell on one group but not the others?"

Torquemada pounded the table again and stood up.

"You will not argue here! You will not ask questions here!" He sat again and glared silently at Pedro for a few moments. "As a Jew, what do you think of Jesus?"

"I love and respect him. He was a brilliant, inspired rabbi."

"Do you think he was the son of God?"

"Yes, just as you and I are sons of God, and everyone else is a son or daughter of God."

"You condemn yourself with every word you speak. Our secretary is recording all of this. Do you want to retract anything?"

"No, I haven't said anything dishonest."

"If you love and respect Jesus, why didn't you become a Christian?"

"Why didn't you? Where in the scriptures does Jesus tell you to torture people and burn them alive?" Where does he tell you to take their property and rob them of their dignity?"

226

Torquemada sprang from his chair and slapped Pedro on the face. A line of blood trickled from Pedro's face, where the priest's ring had cut into the flesh.

"Love your neighbor, love your enemy. Those are the words of Jesus to remember," said Pedro.

Torquemada slapped the other side of his face. "Get him out of here!"

After Pedro was taken out, Torquemada paced in agitation, stopping to stare out the window, oblivious of the other priests. Several minutes passed, and Fray Alonso broke the silence.

"Shall we apply the torture?"

"No, if he repents under torture we'll have to show mercy. I don't want anything to stand in the way of his burning alive. He's the most dangerous man I have ever met."

"All right, Italian, it's all over. You're going home."

A guard opened the heavy door, entered, and removed Guido's chains. "Tell the pope how nice we are to Italians."

As he had planned, Guido had confessed under the threat of torture by fire. Rather than schedule him to join the parade of penitents in the next *auto da fe*, the tribunal decided to send him back to Rome as a gesture of good will to the pope. It was Guido's fanciful hope that he would be set free to spend the rest of his life working contentedly in the vineyards of Tuscany.

"Go with God, my friend," said Pedro as Guido was led out.

"And you, Pedro. With God."

Pedro was overcome with melancholy as he watched a cockroach crawl along the stone floor. People, he mused, are as pathetic as that insect, prisoners on the rack of time, understanding nothing.

That evening a chunk of bread from his supper bowl tasted repellent and he pulled it from his mouth. A note had been wedged into it:

"Do not despair. You will be saved."

Outside the prison, Doña Adelina, the chief jailor's wife, approached Sara in the darkness and introduced herself.

"You must trust me, senora, I'm a devotee of your son and I have a plan to free him, but you must help me."

"Yes! Anything! Tell me what you want me to do."

"Do you have friends or relatives near here?"

"Yes, my brother is on the coast, not far away. He's a ship's captain."

"Good. In ten days, then, one of the guards, who I've bribed heavily, will bring Pedro here before dawn. Can you and your brother be waiting with a coach?"

"Yes. Most certainly. We'll be here. We'll get a coach if we have to build it. But what about the guard? Will they hunt him down and kill him?"

"No, he'll be alright. He's fleeing to France where he was born. At any rate, we all take our chances in this world."

"How can I thank you?"

"By getting him to safety. That's all I want. I must go now. Be here waiting at the right time."

"We will. Bless you."

They hugged and Doña Adelina went back to the prison.

At four a.m. on the appointed morning there was a light rain and a cloudy sky muted the light of the moon. Sara put her hand on her chest to calm the thumping of her heart.

"Mine's pounding too," said Aron. "And I'm sweating like a mule. Look, here they come. That must be them."

Two large figures wearing monk's robes moved toward them hurriedly. "Mama! Aron!" Pedro whispered, "It's me!"

The three embraced joyfully.

"Not to interrupt, but we must leave quickly," whispered the guard. "Please let me come to the coast with you."

"Right," said Aron, "Let's get out of here."

"Where are we going?" asked Pedro.

"To my ship," said Aron, "And then to Tangier to hide out for two months. I've arranged for you to join the crew of a friend, Cristobal Colon, when he sails on a voyage of discovery."

Aron mounted the driver's bench, cracked the whip, and they were off.

On the first day out from Palos, Spain, August 3, 1492, the weather was favorable. A hearty wind blew the three ships steadily on their course toward the Canary Islands. The Nina and Pinta, smaller and faster than the Santa Maria, had to trim sail to stay within sight of Captain-General Cristobal Colon's flagship.

The Basque boatswain Chachu shook Pedro to rouse him before midnight. "Wake up! It's your watch."

Pedro yawned, swiveled off the bunk, and reached for his boots.

On deck, seaman Rico told him all was calm and in order, but cautioned him to keep his eyes and ears open.

"If a sail tears, a line breaks or a storm gathers, wake up the pilot right away."

The watch was uneventful for an hour, until Pedro heard footsteps from the direction of the captain-general's cabin. Cristobal Colon walked toward him carrying a star chart on a lacquered plank.

"A verification, Pedro. I had a dream that the heavens were turned upside down. How could I sleep after that? I know it's foolish but we'd better survey the stars and compare this chart."

"Everything appears to be in the right place."

"So it is. Well, you never know, with dreams. On a voyage to God knows where, we mustn't disregard any omen."

"A wise course, captain."

"You know we're looking for a western route to the Indies. If, as I suspect, we find a tribe of people who speak like characters in the bible, your knowledge of Hebrew will be invaluable."

He gazed into the dark churning water for a while without speaking.

"But truthfully, I have no idea what lies ahead. What do you think of this voyage, Pedro?"

"Certainly it's mysterious, sir, and may we refrain from evil."